OUT OF MIND

OUT OF MIND

J. Bernlef

□

Translated by Adrienne Dixon

DAVID R. GODINE · PUBLISHER
Boston

First U.S. edition published in 1989 by
David R. Godine, Publisher, Inc.
Horticultural Hall
300 Massachusetts Avenue
Boston, MA 02115

Originally published in Dutch in 1984 by Em. Querido's
Uitgeverij B.V. Amsterdam, Holland.

Library of Congress Cataloging-in-Publication Data
Bernlef, J.
[Hersenschimmen. English]
Out of mind / by J. Bernlef : translated from the Dutch by
Adrienne Dixon.—1st ed.
p.   cm.
Translation of: Hersenschimmen.
ISBN 0-87923-734-1
I. Title.
PT5881.12.E73H413   1989
839.3'1364—dc19   87-33824
CIP

First Edition
PRINTED IN THE UNITED STATES OF AMERICA

A touching dream to which we all are lulled
But wake from separately.

Philip Larkin

OUT OF MIND

□ □ □

Maybe it is on account of the snow that I feel so tired. Even in the morning. Vera doesn't, she likes snow. To her there is nothing better than a snowy landscape. When the traces of man vanish from nature, when everything turns into one immaculate white plain: how beautiful! She says it almost in rapture. But this state of affairs never lasts long here. Even after a few hours you see footprints and tire tracks everywhere and the main roads are cleared by snow plows.

I hear her in the kitchen, making coffee. Only the ochre-colored post at the school bus stop still indicates where Field Road passes our house. Actually, I don't understand what has happened to the children today. I stand here by the window every morning. First I check the temperature and then I wait until they turn up everywhere from among the trees in the early morning, with their schoolbags on their backs, their colorful hats and scarves and their shrill American voices. The bright colors make me feel cheerful. Flaming red, cobalt blue. One boy wears an egg-yolk-yellow parka with a peacock embroidered on the back, a boy with a slight limp who is always the last to climb into the school bus. It is Richard, son of Tom the lighthouse keeper, born with one leg shorter than the other. A sky-blue, fan-shaped peacock tail studded with darkly staring eyes. I don't know where they can all be today.

□

The house creaks on its joists like an old cutter. Outside the wind rolls through the crowns of the otherwise bare, bending pines. And at fixed moments, the dull, lowing cry of the foghorn beside the lighthouse on the last rocky spur of Eastern Point. At fixed moments. You can set the clock by it.

Minus three, says the outdoor thermometer, Pop's Heidensieck thermometer, a glass stick in a moss-green protective wooden case, screwed to the window pane. Centigrade to the left, Fahrenheit to the right. Pop and his Heidensieck. He didn't believe in weather forecasting, but he did believe in recording facts. It wasn't for nothing that he had been a court clerk practically all his life. Morning and evening temperatures, noted down in a black marble-grained exercise book. The first and the last thing he did, every day. A kind of ritual. On weekends he took out the exercise book and, sitting at his desk, worked out his graphs on the basis of the recorded temperatures. He kept these graphs, drawn with a hard Faber pencil on salmon-colored graph paper in a folder. Why did he bother with all this? Only once did he ever talk to me about it, shortly before his death, in his cottage close to the inner dunes at Domburg. My time is too short, he said, and the system is too big, too slow and too complex for one man on his own. I merely register facts. But you suspect a system behind those facts, I said. Yes, he said, you might say that. Unless all facts turned out to be aberrations, he added with that thin, ironic little smile of his. But then it would no longer be a system, I suggested. Or a system we cannot have any conception of, he said.

Strange that I should suddenly think of him, as I stand here in Gloucester, on the North Shore of Boston: of my father and his Heidensieck thermometer. Even his grave in the Netherlands must have been cleared by now.

Yes, he used to like systems. As for being fatherly, he would look right over your head, his watery blue eyes fixed on something the rest of us around the table couldn't see. In fact, we were slightly afraid of him, Mama and I. He looked down on us, quite literally. And in a different way as well. If he was in a good mood he would take me out on the balcony in the evening and point out the constellations, the brightly sparkling planet. A few times we saw a falling star. He tried to explain to an eight-year-old that what we were seeing up there in the evening sky was an ancient past, that we were unable to see the real state of the universe, that we could at best calculate it. A number of those stars you could see up there did not really exist any longer, others did. I didn't understand this, but I asked no questions. Such things he said only when he was in a good mood. Usually he sat down at his desk straight after supper and started working. He lived to the age of seventy-four. Three more years and I shall have caught up with him, so far as age is concerned. When Mama died in 1950 he started recording other aspects of the weather, not only the temperature. Snowfalls. Storms. The first signs of spring. The flocks of starlings that flew over his roof in the autumn, that he described as "innumerable" in his almost calligraphic script that so well suited the impersonal nature of his statements. Six years later he, too, died. His heart suddenly stopped. I unscrewed the thermometer from the window frame of his cottage and took it with me. I don't really know why. It is a very ordinary thermometer.

You can always hear Vera coming from afar; the cups and saucers rattle on the tin tray. Aspen-leaf, I sometimes say jokingly to her, but she doesn't think that is very funny. It is caused by a worn neck vertebra, says Dr. Eardly. There is not much you can do about it. Nothing, in fact. Old age.

"Where can the children be?"

"The children? In Holland, of course, where else should they be?"

"No, I mean the ones from here," I point outside. "Cheever's children and the Robbinses and Tom's little Richard."

"But Maarten, it's Sunday today. Come, your tea is getting cold."

How could I have forgotten! And tea? I could have sworn it was morning. But as I look through the other window in the direction of the sea I can tell it must be later. Behind the grey haze lurks a pale sun. It must be this mist that has deceived me. Mist blocks the light. Before sitting down I cast a quick glance at the wall clock. Past three.

I smile at Vera's mocking green eyes with the dark flecks in the pupils. The other day I came across an old photograph of her. She is standing on the deck of the pleasure steamer, leaning with her back against the double white railing. A trip to Harderwijk. The sun shines on her springy hair. It was thick then. She is smiling, you can see her small, regular teeth. The dress she was wearing, I can't remember it now, but it was definitely light in color. I still see us standing on the poop deck together as we sailed out of the harbor. Were we already married then? But the picture I have of her—I mean inside—does not resemble the young woman in the photograph, and not the Vera sitting opposite me either. It is a picture in which all the changes she has undergone have been united. That is why it is more like a feeling than a picture.

Vera. Her abrupt, incomplete gestures; the attentiveness with which she picks a dead leaf from a plant and examines it from every angle, as if to ascertain the cause of death; the way she purses her lips when she is thoughtful, or shakes her head gently when she reads something she finds beautiful. I am the only person who can see in her all the women she has been. Sometimes I touch her, and then I touch all of them at once, very gently. A feeling only she can evoke in me, no one else.

I stir my teaspoon around in my cup, just as she does. A familiar tinkle of metal against thin china.

"Is anything the matter?" she asks. She looks at me scrutinizingly.

"No," I say. "Why?"

"This morning you let your coffee get cold. And I asked you twice to fetch wood from the *boet*. But the only one who came back with a piece of wood in his mouth was Robert."

She laughs. She still has small teeth. But these aren't real ones. She says *boet* instead of shed, because she comes from North Holland, from Alkmaar, just like me. But I simply say shed.

"I felt a bit tired this morning," I say. "I'll get you some in a minute."

"No need, I've already done it myself. You're getting absent-minded, Maarten."

"My memory has never been very good."

I can tell from my voice that I am trying to defend myself against her teasing reproof. "It's because of the snow," I say hurriedly, "the monotony. When everything around you is white, the distinctions fall away. I'm looking forward to spring, aren't you?"

"They've forecast more snow."

"Goodness me."

I fold my hands, look at the tobacco-brown spot of pigmentation between the swollen veins and before I realize it I have said it once more: "Goodness me." It simply slips out.

She puts her head briefly on my head, on my thin hair. When she smiles you can tell she has false teeth. Only when she smiles. Otherwise, her cheeks are still round and almost without wrinkles. In the lobes of her small ears sparkle tiny silver ear-studs, Zeeland ear-studs, from her great-grandmother in Zierikzee.

"Drink your tea."

I drink the tea. Suddenly I feel irritated. I get up and say, "I have to go to the washroom." That's what I used to call it at work. At home I just say "toilet." Of course she immediately notices the difference in nuance.

"Then don't forget to put your gloves on," she says.

I sit here quite often—an old newspaper limp in my hands—when I want to think about something. But the problem is that it is difficult to think about something you cannot remember. Impossible. The morning. Her request, if I would please fetch some wood. Maybe I didn't hear. Although she asked me twice, she said.

I always did have a poor memory. At meetings, my diary was always my indispensable companion. But a whole morning which you have simply forgotten a few hours later? Which has passed by as if it had never been? A minute ago I would have sworn it was an ordinary weekday morning. If Vera had not said anything I might still be standing there now, in the back room, my hands leaning on the window sill, like every morning, looking for the noisy schoolchildren of Eastern Point.

I could have made a better job of those tiles when I put them up. Feel those lumps of cement along the joints. I have always been left-handed, but at kindergarten that was not allowed, cutting with your left hand. The strips for plaiting mats turn out horrid, of uneven width and length. The teacher bends over me. Her dark curly hair tickles my cheek as it brushes past me. "You'd better get the pencil box, Maarten," she says softly, wiping my botched plait-work from the table. I look at the strips of paper at my feet on the floor. Then I get up and open the door.

It is quiet in the corridor. At the end is the storage closet. On the top shelf is the pencil box with its scent of wood shavings and graphite, a smell that comes from deep down in the forest, as old as the earth itself. I have to climb on a chair to look for the box with its compartments of different lengths and widths. Behind me stands Vera, beside the washing machine. I totter and grab the shelf with both hands.

"Stop being so reckless," she says, "and get down from that chair before you fall. What are you looking for?"

"A carpenter's pencil," I mutter as I scramble down. If she asks me again I will say nothing, as if I had not heard her. She does not repeat her question. I walk down the corridor into the living room. The television is on, loud. Vera is slightly hard of hearing. I am not, but sometimes, like just then, it suits me to pretend that my hearing, too, is no longer as sharp as it used to be.

Indeed, what was I doing there? How did I get up on that chair? And so suddenly? All at once I found myself standing on a chair in the laundry room. Without anything leading up to it.

She has put on her lime-green knitted jacket.

"Are you cold?"

"A bit chilly," she says and points out of the window.

It is snowing again. There goes Robert with his nose close to the ground. Following a scent no doubt. I see him disappear among the pine trees behind a rock that sticks slantingly out of the ground. The wind had wiped the snow from the top of the mottled dark grey stone. The veins and cracks on its side show up like a network of fine white lines, a map that I suddenly do not wish to look at. My mouth fills up with spittle.

I swallow. And again. I swallow once more and let my tongue run along my palate. A cheerful female voice announces the four o'clock news. It will probably soon be dark now. I will wait until I see Vera and myself loom up in the blackening plate-glass of the living-room window, as in the frame of a familiar painting. Then I will get up and draw the curtains. I rub my hands together. Yes, that's what I will do, that is what I am going to do.

□

Vera. She has grown thinner. And even smaller, it seems. When she was in her early forties she was almost plump. And then my left hand would run all along her sleeping back until I held one of her breasts in the cup of my hand, gently rubbing the nipple with my thumb. Last summer there was a couple screwing down in the wood near by. She had firm young breasts. I stood watching behind an ash tree. They didn't see me. Dirty old man? No, it wasn't that. The passion of their fierce movements, down there in the tall grass, the girl's curled-up toes and the summer breeze in the tall bracken among the pines behind them. I thought of the gentle, slumbering movements of Vera and me. I was looking at something that I had known but that lay forever behind me. The excitement of the unknown has given way to recognition, the recognition of Vera as she is now, as I have seen her become through the years. With most women of her age the young girl they must once have been cannot possibly be reconstructed. They look as if they have always been like that. But in Vera the features and gestures of the young girl have been preserved like a painting underneath. The reckless speed with which she sits down, even now, the exuberant hand-wave when she sees someone she knows, the outward-pointing feet, a leftover from ballet lessons, the straight neck, despite the wrinkles, still turning as proudly and inquisitively as that of an ostrich.

The house seems bigger than it did once, when Kitty and Fred were still at home. Only Robert goes upstairs now, the ground floor is enough for us. We putter. That is one difference from the past, when you still went to work. You start puttering, you walk around for the sake of walking around. Open a door or closet here and there, and shut it again. For no reason. You see the room, the familiar furniture as it is arranged, the portraits and trinkets, the gleaming glass panes of the dresser in the corner of the room which always reminds me of Grandma's and Grandad's living room, of Grandma's secret store of candy behind a row of snowy-white canisters with their stern black lettering: SUGAR, SALT, CINNAMON, COFFEE. She used to keep thin bars of chocolate there for me, and acid drops or pear drops; words from an improbably distant past, but still with a whiff of their former flavor.

I look around me. Everything has received its own immutable place. You don't throw things away so easily any more, and if you break something you have a feeling other than indifference. You look around you and you know that pretty well all these objects will survive you. They surround you and sometimes you feel: They are looking at me, almost as equals.

"Look at New York!"

It is snowing on the television screen too. A mustard-colored snow plow on Madison Avenue shoves muddy breakers of snow on to the sidewalk. Behind large, illuminated showcase windows, store assistants stand watching. I must not forget to fetch wood from the shed. Those logs are really too heavy for Vera. I haven't sawn and chopped them myself for years. I buy the wood from Mark Stevens, who also supplies Tom at the lighthouse. The fire could do with another log now, though more for the sake of cosiness than for warmth.

I pick up a book from the low round table beside the fireplace. *The Heart of the Matter* by Graham Greene. Never seen that lying here before. It doesn't come from the library either. Almost half-way through the book, a bus ticket peeps out from behind the page, a return ticket, Gloucester-Rockport. I haven't seen Vera reading it. Maybe she borrowed it from Ellen Robbins and that bus ticket is hers. (Why do I so much want this to be the case? Why does this innocent book suddenly seem an intruder?)

Poke the fire, it makes such a lovely shower of sparks. Go on, fly away up the chimney. Out there you'll all be extinguished by the snowflakes with a big hiss. Black dots on the snowy roof, that is all that remains of the falling sparks. I've seen it many times, coming home from a winter walk in the woods with Robert.

Graham Greene. Didn't he write *Our Man in Havana?* I saw the movie once, with Alec Guinness. I remember only a scene of two men playing a game of checkers. But instead of checker pieces they play with small bottles of liquor. Bourbon and Scotch. Every piece that is taken must be drunk. The loser wins.

"Do you remember *Our Man in Havana,* that film with Alec Guinness? Based on a book by Graham Greene?" I deliberately shout a bit, so as to be heard above the television.

"Vaguely," she says, wiping a crumb from the corner of her mouth.

"Based on a book by Graham Greene."

"Could be, yes."

She does not react to the name. Surely it would have been natural for her to say: That's a coincidence, I'm just reading a book by him. Then I would have replied: Not at all a coincidence. I saw that book lying here, and it reminded me of the film. Then everything would tally, our words would fit together like pieces of a jigsaw. But she says nothing.

Walk, I must get up for a moment and walk about. Then it will ebb away again, this feeling of being absent while being fully conscious, of being lost, of losing your way, I don't know what to call this feeling, which can apparently be aroused by the simplest objects like this book.

Robert scratches at the kitchen door. Vera can't hear him. I have to hold the doorknob with two hands against the wind. The dog immediately pushes his cold nose into my outstretched hands. I stroke his tobacco-brown spotted fur in which snow crystals still glisten here and there. Robert knows the way, straight to the crackling fire.

From the kitchen window you can usually see the rocky coast through the trees, and the grey, rolling sea, but today there is nothing in the distance but a black hole. Not even a light anywhere. The fishermen have probably stayed indoors in this weather.

I can see the fishing industry going to the dogs here in Gloucester. The rusty fishing vessels are small, dirty and old-fashioned, and the fishermen haven't the faintest idea of the development of modern, all-automatic fishing fleets on the other side of the globe. I know about it through my work, but I don't tell them. When I occasionally go to the tavern I only listen to their stories. At sea you don't learn how to talk, one of them said to me the other day. You're too busy. And when you're free for a moment there is always the sea about you and you must never take your eyes off it. The IMCO, would that mean anything to them? There is surely nobody who knows it stands for Intergovernmental Maritime Consultative Organization? Not even Vera. She has always said IMCO right from the start, without ever asking what those letters actually meant.

I used to take the minutes at meetings. Later they had a secretary for that, and I switched to doing the catch targets, together with Karl Simic. He never said much. And certainly not about himself, unlike, for instance, Chauvas who always chattered nineteen to the dozen. Catch targets. There were years when I used that phrase every day. No, I don't really think about the office much any more. Occasionally of that tall, skinny Karl Simic, even though he is dead now. Simmitch, that's how you had to pronounce it. A Yugoslav name. He lived on his own in an apartment in Boston. And one morning they found him dead in his bath. When I heard that, I was sorry I had never struck up a friendship with him. But he was just like me: shy and reserved. When we were working you could hear a pin drop.

"What were you doing in the kitchen so long?"

"Catch targets."

"What?"

"Oh, nothing, a phrase from work. I was suddenly thinking of the office. And of poor Karl Simic who committed suicide and none of his colleagues understood why, except me, but I kept my mouth shut. What is left of it all, apart from some faded old minutes and reports full of advice that no one ever took?"

"You men are always so keen on being important and having meetings."

"I was a cog, a well-paid cog, admittedly. But how that intergovernmental machinery fitted together exactly I still don't know to this day."

She has switched off the television. I sit down beside her on the settee. We are silent. Then she puts her hand on my knee.

"You shouldn't always wear the same old pants," she says.

From the front room comes the ringing of a bell. It stops and then starts again. An irritating, intrusive sound. At last it stops.

"Wasn't that the phone?"

"No," I say. "You must have imagined it."

"Maybe it was Ellen Robbins," she says. "She said she might drop by this evening."

She gets up and walks out of the room. I feel an impulse to follow her but, of course, that is silly. She'll be back in a moment. I intertwine my fingers and squeeze them.

It will soon be light outside. If only spring would come soon. Once it is spring again Robert and I can walk on the beach or along the bay. I throw pieces of driftwood into the waves and he brings them back to the beach. A pointless pastime which we both enjoy, each in his own way.

I go to the window and press my nose against the glass. Black. Vera was up first, as usual. She has opened the curtains. I close them again. It's much too early to have them open on such a cold wintry morning. Even the schoolchildren are still in bed. I rub my hands together. Wouldn't mind my coffee now. I sniff. Nothing. She can't have started pouring the water yet. Might as well read a little first.

I take the book from the fireside table and open it where I left off yesterday. I read in bed last night. It happens sometimes that I fall asleep and then the next day I cannot remember what I last read. I leaf back a chapter and put the bus ticket to Rockport inside the front cover.

Vera enters from the room. Not in her navy-blue dressing-gown but in black cotton pants and a loose lime-green jacket over a white blouse. In her hands she is holding long shreds of paper, strips of torn newspaper.

"Did you do this?" she asks.

I shake my head. "Maybe Robert?" I suggest hesitantly.

"Since when do dogs tear newspapers into strips in the toilet?"

She goes to the wastepaper basket beside the piano and drops the paper into it. I watch her and cannot understand why these dumb bits of newspaper make me feel so embarrassed. And it still isn't getting any lighter, it still won't become light.

"If you're closing the curtains, then close all of them," she says. "I'm going to phone Ellen Robbins. It's such foul weather, she'd better not come this evening."

Of course, it is evening. "What's for supper?"

"I'll heat up a pizza. It's Sunday, after all."

"Of course," I say. "Sunday. All right with me."

I try to read the book I am holding in my hands, but the words refuse to form sentences. It is as if I suddenly no longer know English, even though I have been virtually bilingual these last fifteen years. At home we speak Dutch together, but as soon as someone else is present we effortlessly switch over to English. And we often catch ourselves still talking English together long after the guests have left. I stare at the sentences. Slowly they slide back into place. Something flutters to the floor. I bend down and pick it up. An old bus ticket. I put it at the back of the book.

In the front room I hear Vera on the phone.

"Yes, I thought so. But Maarten said I was imagining it . . . That's what I was going to suggest too. We'll be in touch."

I heard her put the receiver down.

"You see, it was the phone just then."

I nod.

"So you did hear it?"

"I remember hearing something," I said, "but I don't think it was the phone."

"But it was."

She goes to the kitchen. I hear her opening the oven door and a moment later the dull plop of the gas leaping into flame. I am still holding the book in my hands. When Vera returns, I say, "Yes, I remember now. Just as I was about to get up, it stopped. That can happen to anyone. Was it Ellen Robbins?"

"Yes, it was Ellen Robbins. She thought we weren't in, that maybe I'd forgotten what we had arranged. Will you keep an eye on the clock? The pizza needs another ten minutes. I'm going to put on a jersey, I keep feeling cold."

I want to ask her, but she has already left the room. Ten minutes. The big hand is now on the seven. When it is on the nine, ten minutes will have gone. But what then? What has to be done? I shut the book and push it away from me. I stare at the black hands of the gold-colored wall clock. There is no second hand on it. It looks as if the clock has stopped. It is a modern one, it doesn't tick.

I go to the kitchen, sit down at the table and look at the bright red kitchen clock on the wall, an electric one with a gold-colored second hand that moves around the clockface with little jerks. I don't let my eyes stray from it for an instant. I have always been a man of the clock. Punctual. That is more than you can say of some people.

One more turn and then the big hand will be on the nine. Then ten minutes will have passed. Time is up. I get up from the chair and go to the living room. "Vera," I call, "time is up." I walk across the room, into the corridor. "Vera, Vera, the ten minutes are up," I call, as calmly as possible.

Then I hear her answer coming from the bedroom. "Turn the oven off then, will you?"

I don't know how fast to get back, to carry out her instructions. When I hear the rushing sound of the gas cease, I sit down at the kitchen table with a sigh of relief. It is only thanks to her answer from behind the closed bedroom door that I have been able to carry out this task. Otherwise I would not have known what to do. It worries me that you can suddenly be so cut off from the most ordinary everyday actions. I have no explanation for it.

Vera is wearing a grey-blue, thick-knitted jersey with a broad, wide-open neck. She has pinned up her hair.

"Why have you put your hair like that?"

"I usually do when I have to do the cooking."

"Do you have to do the cooking now, then?"

"It's already done, really. You're right, it's no more than a habit."

She puts on her flowery kitchen gloves and pulls the baking tray with a pizza on it out of the oven.

"Pizza," I say in surprise.

"Yes," she says, "it's Sunday, after all."

"Pizza day," I nod, and I get up from my chair to fetch plates and cutlery. Vera cuts the pizza into four parts with a meat knife. She flicks two dark bits of meat on my plate.

"Anchovies, I don't like them."

"Pizza," I say, "I like pizza."

"We ought to have a glass of red wine with it," she says. "Do you remember in Rome, by that large square? I can't remember what it was called. There was a big fountain in the middle. We had a pizza so big it didn't fit on the plate. It was hanging all over the sides. Two gypsy beggar girls in those long ragged skirts saw that I couldn't possibly eat all of it and just as I was about to give them each a piece they were ordered off the terrace by one of the waiters. Those indignant dark eyes as they looked over their shoulders when they walked away! Later we saw them on a wide sidewalk in front of another terrace, dancing like two grown-up women. Do you remember?"

"Yes," I say, "Rome. The Trevi Fountain."

"No, that was a different one. That's the fountain you have to throw coins in and make a wish. I wished for a daughter."

"And?"

"I got a son."

I nodded. "There are many fountains in Rome," I say. "I remember. It was before the war."

Vera nods. She has little blushes on her cheeks, from talking, from remembering. I don't quite dare look at her. I spear the leftover piece of pizza on to my fork and hold it so high that Robert has to jump at it with wide-open mouth.

"Pity we have no photographs of that trip," says Vera.

"Yes," I say, "Rome. Rome, city of fountains."

"Three years later it was war."

"All over now," I say. "In the end everything is all over."

I get up to make coffee while Vera washes the plates and puts them in the plate rack. I look sideways at her. She must now be almost as slim again as then, on that vacation in Rome in which I remember nothing. Luckily she told me all about it. My God, what would I do without her?

After coffee we play a game of chess. I give up half-way, I can think of nothing but vanished memories and therefore dare not think of the past any more. Even less talk to Vera about it. Perhaps it is only temporary, perhaps they will come back. Memories can sometimes be temporarily inaccessible, like words, but surely they can never disappear completely during your lifetime? But what are they exactly, memories? They are a bit like dreams. You can retell them afterwards, but what they really are, whether they are real, you don't know, no one does. I have sometimes heard Robert dream, at night, squealing thinly and plaintively from the living room. And sometimes Vera mutters a few words in her sleep, under her breath and unintelligible. I never dream. That is to say, I do not remember having dreamt for ages.

"Do you ever hear me dreaming these days?" I ask. "Aloud, I mean."

"Not that I know," she says. "I suppose I am always asleep myself."

I had hoped I would sleep well last night. Vera slept. She always sleeps soundly, has done ever since she started using sleeping pills three years ago. I was suddenly awake, awake and totally lucid. A branch kept knocking, at ever-lengthening intervals, against the veranda railings. Then even that sound ceased. My head was one large brightly lit space, completely empty. And outside it, there was total calm, winter darkness and Vera's regular breathing.

I got up and sat down at the kitchen table with a glass of milk.

Robert scrabbled out of his basket and stood motionlessly before me for several minutes. "Something is the matter, Robert," I whispered, "you have noticed that correctly, but God knows what it is."

It must be this wretched winter. That is the only thing here, the winters last too long for my liking.

Suddenly Vera is standing before me in her dressing-gown with a face as if fire had broken out. What are you doing here in the dead of night, sitting at the table fully dressed?

Yes, of course, that was rather strange, that I was dressed. I do occasionally get up at night, but I only put on my dressing-gown and my slippers.

I couldn't find my dressing-gown, I said, by way of explanation. She asked if anything was the matter. Nothing, I said, except that my head feels transparent, made of glass or ice, very clear and yet I am not thinking of anything.

Read for a while then, she said, or do the crossword. She pushed the newspaper towards me across the table. You gave me a fright, she said. I wake up all of a sudden and you're no longer there. You shouldn't worry yourself, I said. Take another half of a sleeping pill and go to bed. I'll do the crossword and then I'll go back to bed, too.

Of course it is a stupid pastime, but it makes time fly, I'll say that. I was only partway through when it started getting light. I looked at the clock. Half past seven. Not worth going back to bed. Why not surprise Vera with coffee in bed? I always used to do that on Sundays when I was home from work, from IMCO. Coffee and a roll. And then we'd make love. Not too noisily, because of the children. She would hold me in her hand and circle her thumb over the tip and push it inside herself. That used to be all she needed to do and I'd come, but these days it usually takes much longer. Sometimes too long. Then we both grow too tired to carry on with it and fall asleep again.

She was surprised when I suddenly stood in front of her with the tray. Reinstatement of an old tradition, I said. She sat up. She was wearing a loose black T-shirt that must have been Kitty's. I felt like touching her breasts but I did nothing. I sat down on the edge of the bed and watched how she drank the coffee, with small, careful sips, while holding the cup between her slightly trembling fingers.

She didn't like rolls with aniseed sugar, she said. Anyway, you're supposed to eat them only when there's a birth in the family. I just thought it looked festive, all those colorful grains, I said. And since when did she take sugar in her coffee? Not in the last ten years she hadn't.

Absent-mindedness, I said. Sorry. I was doing the crossword and I wasn't paying attention. So you didn't go back to bed at all? No, I said. Once I start doing the crossword...

I used to be very quick at these things, but last night at the kitchen table nothing would go right. Another word for—another word for—I couldn't think of anything.

There's been something wrong with my thinking recently. Or could it be that my English is at fault? Since my retirement I am at home with Vera practically all day and speak almost nothing but Dutch.

A few times I filled in the wrong word. Deliberately. So as not to do what the puzzle wanted of me. It gave me a brief moment of relief. And I drew a moustache under the Pope's nose, almost without thinking about it, the way I used to scribble matchstick men in the margin of my notepad when taking minutes at meetings. Doodles.

I crumpled up the paper with the puzzle and stuffed it right down to the bottom of the garbage can. No doubt Vera would take all those wrong words badly.

Our house has shiny stained wooden floors with a rug here and there. You only need to go over it with a soft broom and all is clean. Yet the house gets a bit dirtier every year. In corners and grooves burnt-out matches and hard, withered berries and crumbs accumulate. Vera does not seem to notice. Maybe my eyes are better than hers.

Because she is wearing her slippers I cannot hear her walking about now, but otherwise all day we know each other's whereabouts. And Robert, of course, with his sharply tapping claws.

The house no longer creaks, the wind died down last night. Snow is falling again. The thermometer reads exactly zero degrees centigrade.

Vera is wearing her wine-red corduroy jacket and jeans. She has adapted somewhat to the American style of dress. In this country an older person must, at least in terms of clothes, look like a twenty-year-old. I myself stick to the English suits of Dodgson's in Boston. Charcoal grey with a thin stripe. I don't mind if people can tell I don't come from here.

"I'm going out for a little walk with Robert," I say. "When I come back I'll get some wood for the fire."

"Don't forget to put your scarf on," she says, leaning on the broom. Before going out into the hall to put on my coat I kiss her gently on her left cheek.

"You might have shaved," she says, tapping my cheek disapprovingly with a gleamingly lacquered nail.

"Do you know what it is?" I say when I shuffle down snow-covered Field Road with Robert. "It all starts with great, confused feelings."

Later you remember only a kind of fever, a glow from within, which made everything special, the most ordinary things that you walked past together and looked at and talked about with her. A barn, a notice board, a flock of starlings flying up from a field. You felt a longing to absorb everything she looked at, to forget nothing, not one moment of this world that had suddenly become her world: cool, bright, unfathomable.

You should never go back to places you used to know. If you do, you destroy that glow, the core of your memories, like Father, who, old as he was, took the car after Mama's death and went back to all the houses in which he had lived with her. A few had been torn down, strangers were living in others, behind pleated net curtains and thick-leafed potted plants on the window sill. He said that after his journey his memories seemed more like fiction than fact, and he felt bitter because the world had changed and had not taken account of his past and his loss.

"So, don't look back!" I say to my dog and I forgot to put on my scarf, after all. Vera is sure to have found out long ago. Sometimes she thinks I deliberately disregard her advice, but that is not so.

All around us, snow falls in thuds from wide-spreading fir branches. When the sun comes out presently, there may well be a thaw. High above us a few seagulls zigzag, but in the woods not a bird stirs. Wherever you go, around here, you smell the sea. A strong smell of algae, seaweed and fish, mingled with the mild, rising scent of millions of brown, decomposing pine needles.

We turn left into Fort Hill Avenue and arrive at Eastern Point Boulevard. Across the bay, the wooden houses of Gloucester on their stone foundations lie scattered against the hillsides, painted in the same cheerful colors as the fishing boats: moss-green, dove-grey, flamingo-pink or brick-red. The two sky-blue, bell-shaped spires of the church high above Main Street seem to keep watch over all those scattered snowy roofs. Between the blue spires stands a life-size statue of the Madonna, holding instead of the Baby Jesus, a schooner in her left arm. Our Lady of Good Voyage.

Every now and then cars and pick-up trucks drive past slowly. The drivers greet me, although they don't always know me. Fifteen years ago Vera and I came to live here. The house belongs to IMCO. An ex-secretary lived in it before, Joseph Stern. After that it was empty for a year. No one wanted to live so far from work. I didn't mind traveling to Boston every morning on the little train. Maybe the oldest and most ramshackle train in the United States, with such dirty windows to the carriages that you could hardly see that you were riding through the back yards of the wooden houses of Salem. In the summer I would watch half-naked toddlers, playing in brightly colored inflatable bathing pools, in winter the garden furniture would be stacked away and covered in snow. The wooden seats in the train were hard—there was no first-class carriage here—but the journey lasted no longer than an hour and almost all the time closely followed the coastline of marshy inlets full of grassy tussocks, islets and small bays with marinas, wooden jetties and summer cottages along the banks. It was a friendly journey through a friendly world.

When I retired, IMCO allowed me to stay in the house. It was never really mentioned. I simply continued to pay the rent to a real-estate office in Boston and as for the rest, nothing changed.

You get cold feet in the snow, no shoes are proof against it. "Come," I say to Robert who plods faithfully beside me, "we'll go a bit faster."

Many of the clapboard houses around here are empty in the winter. They belong to rich people from Boston and these days even from New York, who come here in the summer to go sailing and fishing. The clocks stand still in the empty rooms and only a magazine or a newspaper on a table indicates that people lived here last year.

Denial. Of course! Another word for refusal. Six letters beginning with d. I'd been chewing on that for a whole hour. It is as if the winter air is widening my veins. Maybe that's what it is, hardening of the arteries. You become forgetful. It's part of old age.

Year by year things happen to your body. Your feet lose their springiness. You go up and down the stairs once and you have to sit down to catch your breath. Your eyes start to water when you look at one spot for a long time. The shopping bag moves more and more often from one hand to the other and you meet fewer and fewer people's eyes. But this is different. More a general feeling of unease than a specific symptom. But no, it would be nonsense to think there is something really wrong. "I'm still going strong!"

I must not make a habit of this, of talking aloud to myself, especially not now that Robert and I are approaching the inhabited world. Robert dashes through a white open gate, and down a garden path. Must have smelled another dog. He disappears behind a house. I walk on. He'll catch up with me soon enough.

Now you can see the harbor clearly, cutting deep into the land; the concrete landing stages and the cranes in front of the fish factories and cold stores. Here and there, rows of wooden poles of former landing stages stick criss-cross out of the water, in some places still connected by cross-beams.

Cod and lobster. Lobsters as big as your head. Thanks to the tourists there is still a bit of a living to be made here. And some export to Boston and New York in those large, silver-colored freezer trucks that drive back and forth every day.

I don't have much to do with life as such any longer, but I still enjoy observing all these daily activities. There's not much going on at home these days. That is why you have to get out, not sit indoors all the time. Your world would shrink too fast.

In the past a ferry used to cross from here to the other side but now you have to walk all the way round the harbor to reach the town. And the nearer you get to the center the more steeply the road climbs. I am beginning to feel my legs. If the tavern is open I'll take a rest there.

Change has struck in the tavern, too. Where six months ago there was still a pool room with six of those green meadows on bulbous brown legs, slightly mysterious under low-hanging steel lamp-shades, there is now a stage crammed with sound equipment and microphones. There is probably dancing here on Saturdays. But the long bar is still the same. I look around. The barmaid is standing by the cash register with her back towards me.

When she turns to face me I have to hold on to the raised rounded edge of the bar with both hands. I order a draft beer.

Of course, I must have changed a great deal in fifty years. Grown fatter. Her nails are painted bright red. The nature of the work requires it. When the phone rings I hear that her voice is deeper, rawer. From smoking, of course. Even in those days she used to smoke a pack a day. Beautiful firm round buttocks. Again she turns, still speaking in the phone. Her eyes meet mine, then rove further away, around the empty café. When she has finished phoning, she puts a cassette into the recorder. I ask her if she would please turn the music off. There is already so much noise in the world. I won't say anything about the restlessly flickering but soundless television, obliquely to my right, on a protruding shelf above the bar. It is the sun of every establishment, determining the customers' visual focus and food for conversation.

She nods briefly and does what I have asked her. When my glass is empty she looks at me questioningly. The same light-brown eyes and high cheekbones. Of course it can't be her. I can do nothing but nod, caught once again in that gaze (it can't be her, do you hear, it simply can't be, everyone grows older, excepting no one, no one). She puts a full glass on the coaster and takes some money from the little heap of change in front of me.

Even these days I still think of her sometimes, the way we used to walk along the straight North-Holland canal where, hidden behind a dike, lay her parents' weekend cottage to which she took me to make love for the first time.

Someone enters, a young man in navy-blue turtleneck sweater and jeans. She calls him by his name, Geoffrey. They talk about the band that is coming to play here on Saturday. I don't need to say anything. I only listen and look at Karen, who changes into a girl whom the boy calls Susan and who is then suddenly, in a flash, briefly Karen again, the Karen of fifty years ago, who used to shrug her shoulders in just the same way, the left one slightly higher than the right.

Geoffrey orders a Budweiser which he drinks straight from the bottle. He cracks a joke and as he puts the bottle back on the counter he briefly touches her cheek. She pushes his hand away laughingly, but not too decisively.

Maybe I was too timid. Maybe that was why I lost her. What are you lying there looking at me for? I'm happy you're so beautiful. Let me feel it. And I had to act the lover while I was really still a little boy. With his first girl, every boy must conquer his mother, those big warm breasts between which you rubbed your face, those nipples you sucked at as a greedy baby, who knows, from some primeval memory.

I look at the girl called Susan. How often have I thought of this: to meet Karen once more. For a moment they seemed to fit into each other, this barmaid at the tavern and she. I get up and leave. When she calls after me that I have forgotten my change I merely wave my left hand dismissively above my head, as though wishing, by that gesture, to banish the comparison for ever from my thoughts.

I walk up the steeply climbing Hancock Street and Dale Avenue, past neatly cared-for houses with their wooden, empty conservatories and doorsteps swept clear of snow, until I reach Prospect Street. At the back of the Maplewood sweet shop two women in unbuttoned coats are eating cream cakes.

Philip sat reading behind his overcrowded desk in the second-hand bookstore. He calls me by my surname. Hello, Mr. Klein. I go up to him and he looks a bit surprised when he feels my firm handshake. I nod contentedly. Philip scratches his ginger chin-strap beard, apologizes that there is no hot coffee left, and the asks how I liked *The Heart of the Matter* by Graham Greene.

The question takes me aback. I am not ready for it. It also seems as if I only half understand it. Like an incomplete sentence. You can guess at the rest, but there are more possibilities.

"Haven't got round to it yet," I say, and in order to please him I select another book by the same author from one of the shelves. *Our Man in Havana.*

"I saw the movie once," I explain, "with Alec Guinness." He nods but I can tell from his face that he doesn't know the movie. I pay. He accompanies me to the door and holds it open for me.

"Next time I'll stay longer," I say. "I like the air here, that smell of old paper and dust and printer's ink."

I put the paperback in the inner pocket of my lined coat. Through small side-streets I zigzag slowly and carefully downward, in the direction of the bay and the harbor. I walk down Western Avenue. There are large houses here, villas with wood carvings not confined to the eaves but also enclosing the windows in fanciful chalice shapes. The sea is as calm and mouse-grey as the sky. The sou'wester of the fisherman's statue on its plinth is rimmed with snow and the spokes of the ship's wheel, which he grasps with both hands as he peers towards his shipwrecked mates at sea, also carry thin white edges of snow.

A car stops at the curb right in front of me. Through the rear window I see Robert, nervously turning on his axis. Vera leans sideways and immediately starts talking to me in an agitated voice while she holds the door open for me.

"I've been sick with worry. Robert came home on his own. I thought you'd had an accident. I've been driving all over until at last I saw you walking here. How could you forget the dog, Maarten? And then coming all this way. A little walk, you said."

"I went to the bookstore," I say airily. "Bought another book by Graham Greene. *Our Man in Havana.* The one they made that movie of, with Alec Guinness, you remember?"

Her mouth sets in irritation. "If you intend to stay away half the day you could at least tell me."

I remain silent. Of course she is right. Robert lays his damp snout on my shoulder and then presses it against my cheek. We drive along the shore. The lights across the bay flicker in a long, faintly curved line. And there, far away at the furthest tip, the illuminated cone of the lighthouse scans the black water at regular intervals. I look at it until a bend in the road removes it from my field of vision. Then we drive home in silence past a wall of snow-covered pine trees.

How dark it has suddenly become. The feeling of anxiety has come back, as if I had been deceived by something or someone today, led up the garden path. When we stop on the gravel in front of the veranda, I quickly got out and open the door on the other side for her. I take her brown purse from her and say, "I am very sorry, Vera, really I am." I follow her and Robert into the house, which briefly stares at me with all its black windows at once.

What worries me most of all is that the dog did not go in search of me, did not follow my trail. Could Robert have smelled something about me? Something that made him decide firmly to turn back and go home on his own?

"It's the winter," I say to Vera, "this damned long, rotten winter," while I help myself to more French beans and sprinkle some salt over them. "This winter is making me restless, fidgety."

"I was only getting worried," she says.

With two outstretched fingers I touch her cheek. "I love you, Vera."

She nods absent-mindedly, as if what I said didn't quite sink in.

"Do you remember us walking there, hand in hand, along the canal, on the old back dike? Below us on the other side lay the *polders* and in between there was a ditch with willows along it. We walked above the land, above the red pantiled roofs of the laborers' cottages and farmhouses. Suddenly a splash of sunlight fell from a hole in the clouds right on a group of black-patched cows that went on grazing unperturbed. We stood still on the dike, you and I. You put your arm around my waist. A hole in the clouds, isn't that what you call it? A frayed hole that very slowly closed again from the edges inward. We looked at it, from where we were standing, high above the land, you and I, and then we kissed."

"I don't know what you are talking about, Maarten."

I purse my suddenly cork-dry lips. I look at the dull yellow shine of the reading lamp and make a movement as though chasing a fly from my forehead. Then I desperately grab hold of the edge of the table.

"You are tired," she says. "I can tell that. You slept badly last night, you've been walking around all day. That's why it is. Now why don't you go and shave before Ellen Robbins comes."

"Ellen Robbins?" I startle at the sudden uncontrolled aggression in my voice.

"Maarten, she comes here so often."

I nod. Ellen Robbins. Of course. She sails into the room like a battleship.

"Why are you laughing?"

"Ellen Robbins sailing into the room, I mean, coming into the room like a battleship sailing into port." For a moment I have to laugh so much that the tears spring to my eyes.

"What makes you say that?"

"Nothing. You have to admit she doesn't exactly move like a ballet dancer."

Now Vera also laughs a little, fortunately. I look around the room, let my eyes glide along the gleaming furniture, the black piano. Everything is in order again, back in its place. We are sitting opposite each other by the table, Vera and I, a burning lamp hangs above us and just now we laughed together. I take her right hand, rub gently over the wedding ring which she can easily take off these days. Once they had to saw it off her finger when she had to have an operation.

"Do you remember," I say, "when you had to have that operation on your stomach, that this ring was stuck rock fast to your finger? It wouldn't come off no matter how they tried."

"Don't pull so hard. That's twenty years ago."

"There's something I have to do," I say. I rub my hand contentedly, "But what?"

"Shave," she says.

I shake my head. "That too. Ultimately . . ."

A word I rarely use, ultimately. A word from work, which I occasionally throw out at meetings as a life-buoy to one of my colleagues if he becomes entangled in a complicated argument. Ultimately . . . A formulation suggesting a summary that never comes. A moment of helplessness for a speaker, which causes the people around the table to avoid one another's eyes in embarrassment. Bahr, Chauvas, Johnson and that haggard-looking Karl Simic.

I walk out of the room, up the stairs. While I am shaving I shall no doubt remember what else I have to do. Robert is waiting for me at the top of the stairs. He walks ahead of me, his claws tapping on the linoleum. A dog knows your life patterns, knows exactly what you are going to do. I grope for the light switch in the bathroom but I cannot find it. Why is it so dark everywhere around here? Vera shouldn't be so stingy with the light.

"Maarten," she calls from downstairs. "What are you doing up there?"

I suddenly remember. Fetch wood. Of course!

"Come on, Robert, we'll get some wood from the shed. Come on."

Quickly I go down the stairs. Vera stands waiting for me below, her hands on her hips.

"Out of the way!" I call out jokingly as I take the last step. "Robert and I are going to get you some wood."

"There's plenty of wood left," she says, taking hold of Robert's collar. "What were you doing upstairs?"

"Upstairs is part of the house too," I say, a little sheepishly.

"We never go up there any more, you know that very well. And please go and shave. I don't want Ellen to see you like this."

I go into the bathroom. Robert has gone with Vera. He knows he always gets something from her. From me he gets only wood. A stick to run after on the beach or in the woods.

I look at my face in the mirror over the washstand. No one can tell from it what I used to look like. Not even I myself. Be that as it may . . . I wet my face, squirt a blob of shaving cream on my fingertips and with the fingers of my left hand rub the slithery foam over my cheeks and chin.

You must make sure to pull the skin straight, otherwise the blade gets caught in the wrinkles. Black dots in white shaving floss swirl around in the wash bowl and then disappears down the drain. Beard hair. Another word for beard. Moustache, goatee, whiskers. Uncle Karel had whiskers. Until May 15, 1940. When the Netherlands capitulated, Uncle Karel shaved off his proudly up-twirled whiskers. In protest. A first and last act of resistance. At the bank where he worked everyone understood at once. First they had looked surprised when he came in with a bare face. He had run two fingers of his right hand over his upper lip and then, somewhat apologetically, shrugged his shoulders. Everyone had understood, he said. The Germans. Damned Huns. The Queen gone to England. And so the only thing Uncle Karel could do was shave off his whiskers. Almost a logical consequence of history.

"There, now you look smart again, Maarten."

Don't talk to yourself. At least not when other people can hear you. When you talk you should be addressing another person, not yourself.

It is as if I can hear two voices, women's voices. Surely we don't have company? Maybe the radio.

Cautiously I open the door and go into the hall. Vera's voice. I try not to listen to what the voice in the living room says, and press my nails into the palms of my hands. I stand very still.

"I'm really worried. You can't see there's anything wrong with him. But that makes it all the more alarming. Sometimes he tells me things about us that I was never part of . As if I were a different person in his eyes. And then suddenly he can't remember a whole chunk of his own past. I feel so helpless because I don't know how to help him. And it has happened so suddenly. Practically overnight he has become like this."

Vera shouldn't worry herself so. I quickly enter the room and then stop in my tracks, stiff with fright.

A big robust woman is sitting in my place at the table. A stern female in a mouse-grey suit and black hair in a bun with a wooden pin stuck through it on the back of her head. She says my name and then I recognize her. Of course.

"Hello, Ellen," I say, timidly as a child, and spontaneously shake hands with her. As if by this gesture I want to make amends for having stared at her without recognizing her just now.

"How formal we are today, Maarten," she says. She laughs and Vera laughs a little too. Maybe everything is funny, although I cannot see what exactly there is to laugh at. But be that as it may . . .

"How is Jack?" I ask.

Their faces stiffen. Mysterious, how quickly people's facial expressions can change. You can't read thoughts. Language says you can, but reality is different. Faces are like the surface of the sea. They change constantly under the influence of countless contrary and invisible undercurrents.

"I always recognize people best by their voices," I say. "I have a bad memory for faces, but voices I recognize at once."

The conversation must proceed. Their faces, on either side of the round patch of light from the lamp, still wear that rigid, plaster-cast expression.

"And when someone is dead," says Ellen Robbins. Her voice trembles and Vera puts her hand on Ellen's arm in a protective gesture.

"Cassettes, tapes," I continue. "Lots of people do that these days. For later. You hear someone's voice and his whole person reappears before your eyes. Because of the sound of his voice you see him again altogether. Down to the smallest detail."

It's no good. I can tell, they don't want me to be with them. I turn away and go to the back room, to the piano. I sit down on the stool. I place my fingers in a chord on the keys and suddenly it is as if my whole body fills up with meaningful knowledge again. I begin to play, the adagio from Mozart's fourteenth piano concerto. For how long have I known this by heart? What does that mean, knowing music "by heart?" It is a knowledge you cannot picture, or put into words, but which pours straight, without the intervention of language and thought, from your fingers into the instrument.

In the other room I hear two women talking softly to each other. I take some music from the top of the piano and place it open on the music stand. The first minuet from the fourth English Suite by Bach.

Greta Laarmans always used to rap me on the knuckles here. You're not playing what it says. I can still play, but the tempo has gone. My playing sounds hesitant and slow, heavy and clumsy. I ought to practice more. Suddenly all the pleasure ebbs away from my hands. I press the pedal and let the notes die down in the middle of the minuet. For a long time I stare at the black and white notes, fixed between the staves and bars in the music book. Then I close the lid.

It is silent in the house. Can Vera have gone to bed yet? It happens sometimes that I play for a while at night, before going to sleep. Vera likes it when I play while she is dozing in bed or reading, the book propped against the white bedside table, the little round reading glasses low down on her nose.

It is only seven o'clock on the wall clock. Must have stopped. There is a clock in the kitchen too, an electric one.

Vera is standing in the kitchen, wearing an apron. She stirs a steaming pan of soup with a wooden spoon. I look at the bright red kitchen clock.

"I'm not hungry," I say. "It's only seven o'clock. I see, but it feels much later."

"That's because you're tired," she says, stirring all the while. "You didn't sleep well and you've been out for a long walk. Why don't you go to bed?"

"Children's bedtime," I say. I meant it as a joke but the words came out quite differently. As if I were talking to children, real children, who whine to be allowed to stay up longer. (I used to have children myself, Kitty and Fred. I raised them and now they are gone, you never see them any more . . .)

As a child you often had that. You'd wake up in the morning and the walls of your room were all wrong around you. In your mind you had to swivel the room around so that everything would be in its proper place again and you were able to get up and go out of the door, into the day.

With my hands clasped under my head I look at the azure-blue cotton bedroom curtains, while in my thoughts I put the rooms of the house back into place. Vera must already be up, although I can hear no sound. The light, even though muted by the curtain, is bare and hard. It must have snowed again in the night, I think.

I get out of bed and open the curtains. It doesn't look as if any new snow has fallen. Robert's footprints lie sunk deep in the snow, less sharp at the edges than would have been the case with fresh prints. The tops of the pine trees point motionlessly into the sky like broomsticks. A narrow path has been trodden from the porch to the moss-green shed in the right-hand corner at the far end of the yard.

I brush my teeth and search meanwhile for words, a formulation of what I feel. As if inside me there were someone who remembers another house, the interior arrangement of which sometimes cuts across that of this house. Rooms ought to be absolute certainties.

The way in which they lead into one another ought to be fixed once and for all. You should be able to open a door as a matter of course. Not in fear and anxiety because you don't have the faintest idea of what you may find behind it.

I am standing in front of the clothes closet. For today I chose the black suit I bought at Rowland's in Lafayette Street. Because of its deep inside pockets. Even my desk diary fits in them. I can feel something in the left-hand inside pocket.

A picture postcard of a dazzling white-washed Mexican church. The sun must be straight overhead because there is no shade to be seen. The open door is a vaulted black hole. *Love—Kitty.* A six-year-old postmark. Clearly a joke on the part of some colleague. Wouldn't surprise me if it was Maurice Chauvas. Always full of tales about his escapades. He knows I don't like such jokes. Probably thinks Vera checks through my pockets when I come home from the office. I pull a belt through the loops of my pants, buckle it, and leave the bedroom. Since I have given up beer I have lost a good deal of weight.

Vera must have left for the library by now. On Monday and Wednesday mornings she works there as a volunteer. Writing out cards. They still do that by hand there. She has the handwriting for it. Small, upright and clear.

I go to the kitchen and open the door of the refrigerator, which switches on at once as though wishing me a humming, throbbing good morning.

Once you start eating there is no stopping. Chewing does you good. You should always chew well, slowly, until everything is mashed up small. Only then must you swallow. This chicken tastes bad. Here you are, Robert. I toss him some cleaned-off bones. Let's have a look what else there is. Liver pâté and a slice of cool pineapple out of a can. Robert is still hungry too. He can have half of this box of cookies, but no more. I'll eat the rest. It's bad to go to work on an empty stomach. Moreover, I am always afraid they'll hear my insides rumble during a meeting. Insides. When you think of that, and you look down the gleaming polished table and you see them all sitting there in their suits, with their papers in front of them, and inside those suits it is full of blood and meters of coiled intestines and a pumping heart, when you think of that, you can hardly stifle your laughter. Nice, this ice-cold orange juice, straight from the bottle into your mouth. Some of it spills, but who cares? A quick wipe with a kitchen cloth and you're spick and span again.

"Come on, Robert, it's getting late. We'll clean up the mess later."

How often have I told Vera not to touch my desk? My briefcase is standing underneath it in its proper place, but where are my papers? Maybe they'll be handed out at the meeting. That often happens at special unscheduled meetings. I'd better take the case all the same, because there are sure to be more papers. Producing documents, we're good at that at IMCO. Reports about the catches of the last quarter, forecasts about the migration of salmon. For as long as I have been working at IMCO these have never yet come true. Only lobster is reliable, both in its movements and its numbers. But then, why should fish bother themselves about a bunch of gentlemen somewhere high and dry in an office block in Boston, who want to share out the catches more or less fairly among the different countries of the world? If you start thinking along those lines, Leon Bahr once said to me, you might as well stay at home. So we don't. We bend over computer tables, models and scenarios, and the stacks of papers grow and the fish in the seas swim and swim and have no inkling of our existence.

□

Hunting for things. If there's anything I detest that's it. Where are my keys? And what imbecile has locked all the doors? Robert follows me like a good dog as I try the kitchen door, the laundry-room door and the outside door. Vera must have double-locked it. How could she be so silly?

I go to the phone and call the library. To a girl's voice I explain who I am and ask if I can please speak to my wife, that it is very urgent because I have to set off for work very soon to attend an important meeting. She asks me to hold the line a moment, but the moment lasts so long that I finally throw the receiver furiously back on its cradle. I have to get to that meeting. Now. Without a secretary they are nowhere.

On the shelf in the laundry room I find what I am looking for at once. I take a screwdriver and hammer from the wooden toolbox and go to the door.

It is easier than I expected. I wedge the screwdriver between the door and the post. After a few hammer blows the door leaps open towards me. Robert slips out immediately and barks, relieved that he, too, has been freed from his imprisonment.

I quickly return to the hall, put on my coat and collect my briefcase into which I tuck the screwdriver and hammer for the time being. It is quarter to eleven, I see in passing. I must hurry.

Robert likes nothing better than a walk. He runs ahead of me, sometimes to the right, then again to the left of the path, into the snowy wood, and waits for me further on, with steaming mouth and wagging tail.

This is not an official road but a neighborhood path. It runs past the Cheever's brick house and the untidy wooden affair of Pat and Mark Stevens. Their garden is one big junk yard. Today there is a half-demolished bright-red pick-up truck without wheels, which, to judge by the black letters on the door, once belonged to Nortons Hardware Store. Just beyond Pat's and Mark's house the woods end and the dunes begin. They are the color of bleached corduroy. Or matting. The wind has blown ripples in the snow at the foot of the dunes. Like congealed waves. I am the first to arrive, I can tell from the virgin snow all around. It is perhaps a rather strange and yet quite suitable place for an IMCO meeting, so close to the sea. Robert dashes up a dune, but you needn't think, Robert, that those two crows will let themselves be caught by you.

He lives in the same world as I, and yet he must experience it quite differently. This can be inferred from his behavior. Close above the ground there must hover a world of scents which he crosses this way and that, sniffing excitedly. His tracks are recorded in the snow. To me they seem a purposeless network. Nothing but consequences. Not a cause to be found anywhere, let alone a system.

I know my way around here. If I bear left, past three planted rows of marram, I will reach a shell path that leads straight to the slate-gray house where the meeting is to be held.

I climb the snow-blown steps to the veranda and peer in. A white lacquered table with four chairs around it. This is where it is. I am not surprised I am the first to arrive—I always am. I have never yet seen Bahr turn up on time, even though he is the chairman. Johnson and Simic always phone to say they are on their way and Chauvas cracks jokes about his dates that are forever getting out of hand. I do not record the times of their arrival, only the time at which Bahr opens the meeting. A subtle reference to the official starting time mentioned at the top of the agenda. But today there is no agenda, so the gentlemen are clearly not bothered about punctuality.

Beside the grass-green door is a brass bell. I press it but hear nothing. I put my ear against the door and press again. Bell out of order. I turn. Robert is standing on the snow-covered porch, wagging his tail. A few seagulls float on invisible thermal waves over the undulating dune ridge. Not a soul to be seen. Anywhere.

I open my briefcase and take out the screwdriver and hammer. This time it is much more difficult. The hammer blows sound loud, hard and dry, and from time to time I glance briefly over my shoulder, because for the secretary to a meeting to be forcing a door open is not an everyday event, I realize that.

It is very cold in here. No sign of any heating. Robert wanders into the kitchen but there is nothing there except an empty tea canister on the granite draining-board. An almost hostile, bare interior. What possessed them to choose this place as a venue? Or could I have misunderstood? Mistaken the date perhaps? Were documents sent out and did I not receive them for some reason or other?

I sit down at the table and look out of the window across the snow-covered dunes. In the summer I love this landscape with its somewhat pale, scrubbed colors and tough shrubs and stubborn thistles, the wind moving through the rows of marram on the flanks of the dunes. But today my eyes confront a bare and indifferent terrain. The sky above is gray and closed. Damned winter.

I know a secretary belongs and yet does not belong. He is a marginal figure, really. But when they arrive I shall have a piece of news for them. I shall get up when they come in. I'll wait for them to sit down, get out their papers and arrange them in front of them on the table. Then I'll get up and beg permission to speak.

"Gentlemen. For some considerable time I have had my doubts about the effectiveness of our meetings. You know as well as I do that the recommendations regarding each quota (for they are no more and can be no more than recommendations) are being evaded by the countries concerned, who hire ships under foreign flags. The statistics and catch figures of the past year do not comform with reality and besides, no fish has ever let itself be guided in its movements by our computer forecasts. None of this is news to you, although we try anxiously to conceal the relative futility of our organization from the outside world and from each other. However, another factor has now come into play: the fully automatic fishing fleet, originating from Japan. You are surprised? I am sure you are, but if you will allow me to explain.

"First, with the aid of hydrophones, the sounds emitted by feeding fish are recorded under water. These recordings are then played back under water by means of powerful loudspeakers. In this way, fish are lured over great distances to a particular area where a completely mechanized fishing fleet, steered by remote computer control, is in attendance. The fleet uses electrical nets. An electric field is set out in the sea. Any fish entering this field becomes paralyzed and is sucked into the holds by means of enormously powerful pumps."

A feeling of nausea suddenly comes over me. I just manage to reach the porch. As I hang over the railing my stomach empties itself into the snow, a mucky brown, steaming pulp in which even Robert shows no interest. I feel cold.

What am I doing here? In the summer, people from Boston live here, a bald man and his small dark wife. Fortunately the door can still be shut in such a way that from the outside you can hardly tell it has been forced open. I may get into trouble over this. Without looking back I walk down the shell path, in the direction of the sea. If I return along the beach there is little chance that anyone will see me. Let's hope it will soon start snowing again and all my footprints will be covered up.

I want to get back to Vera. I want to hold her close and say I am sorry. And that she shouldn't leave me alone like this. All these terrible things happen because I am being left alone.

"Come on, Robert, we must go home at once."

A sharp wind and the sound of the sea swishing, sighing over the smooth hard sand. I watch the foaming, advancing water. Underneath, a counter-current pulls it swiftly over the sand, back to the sea. If I look at these opposing currents for a long time I grow dizzy.

Most people talk about the "salty sea air," but I call it the "white scent." Those little birds the color of brown rope, tripping along the tide line, would probably understand what I mean.

I am beginning to regain my feeling, my normal feeling. As if my blood is beginning to flow again. I should take such a brisk walk more often. I used to, in the winter, with Pop. Warmly dressed on our bikes along the Bergen Road to Bergen-Binnen where we would stop for a bowl of pea soup, and then straight on to the beach. There we would put our heavy bikes in the store room of a first aid station and walk all the way to Egmond and back. The Dutch wind was nastier, more biting than this one.

I can see the tall white flagpole of the Atlantic Motel sticking out above the last ridge of dunes. Robert knows exactly which way to go. The wooden steps to the beach are half buried by snow, but the handrail shows precisely where they are. Robert sniffs at a yellow plastic crate that juts out of the sand.

On the Atlantic Road I have to pause to catch my breath. Robert keeps running around me impatiently. Then we walk back towards home with the sea and the wind at our backs. As we pass the Cheevers' brick house I call Robert to heel. Before you know where you are he has disappeared, in search of Kiss, the Cheevers' white Pomeranian.

Vera's light-blue Datsun is parked in front of the porch. I climb the steps and look through the window. She is on the phone. I tap against the glass but she doesn't hear. Then she suddenly sees me. Startled, she drops the phone. I wave and enter the house through the open front door.

When I enter the front room she is sitting by the table with clasped hands. Her face looks helplessly at me, like that of a child who waits anxiously for what the grown-ups have in store for her this time. "Let me take your coat." She has to stand on tiptoe to help me out of my coat. I sit down by the table while she puts my coat away. She returns with a book in her hand, a paperback with a green cover. A man in a raincoat looks sideways at a brilliantly lit hotel on top of a hill. The title is *Our Man in Havana*.

"Is it about Cuba?" I enquire. I know Vera is interested in politics. She is about to answer but changes her mind and sits down again, placing the book upside down on the table.

"Maarten," she says, "where have you been?"

I take a deep breath of relief. "A long walk," I say. "I have decided to go for long walks more often in future. It's good for the circulation. You should have come with me but you had already gone when I left. Where have you been?"

"I've been to see Dr. Eardly."

That gives me a fright. "There's nothing wrong with you, is there?"

She puts her hand on mine. "I went for you, Maarten. You are so restless these days. You do things and the next moment you can't remember having done them. Strange things. I went to talk about it with Dr. Eardly."

"I feel perfectly healthy. Strange things? What kind of strange things?"

"When I got home the whole kitchen was strewn with chicken bones."

"Robert," I say hesitantly.

"Half a chicken, Maarten. In the morning, on an empty stomach, you ate half a chicken. And a can of liver pâté. And several pineapple rings and a box of cookies."

"A healthy appetite for an old man, that's all I can say."

"It's no laughing matter, Maarten. But Dr. Eardly says we can do something about it together. And he's given me tablets for you, for the night."

"I sleep very well, actually."

"Sometimes you get up in the middle of the night. You get dressed. You don't know the difference between day and night any longer."

"It's all because of this damned winter," I mutter. I look at her earnestly, almost severely, as if wanting to persuade her . But what I am really doing is begging her to understand something I don't understand myself. Something that suddenly comes over me and vanishes equally suddenly, leaving a dark shadow of panic behind, which slowly ebbs away until only that slight sense of unease remains that I now feel almost the whole day.

"I know what the trouble is," I say, "Chauvas said the same to me at a meeting the other day. 'My dear Maarten,' he said, 'don't you remember we discussed that in detail at our last meeting? Look it up in your own minutes.' I've been a bit forgetful for a long time."

"It was four years ago you last went to an IMCO meeting," she says.

"Sure, sure," I say. "Did you really think I didn't know that?"

"You should take it easy, Dr. Eardly said. You should stay indoors for the time being. Your memory is a bit confused. We must steer the past back into its proper channels. Together. Our past, Maarten."

"Don't look so sad, Vera," I say. "There are lots of things I do remember."

"I can help you," she says softly. "We've been together almost fifty years. Dr. Eardly said it will be all right again."

"What does this Dr. Eardly know about me? I've been to see him twice maybe in all the years we've been living here."

"Don't get excited. He promised to call in one of these days."

"Doctors," I sneer. "Especially in this country with its obsession with health. They do nothing but keep the pharmaceutical industry on its feet, the pill manufacturers."

"Don't excite yourself so."

"That's what you said before."

"I know."

"What should I do, then?" My voice sounds dull and timid, as though admitting I am sick. Therefore I say, by way of compensation, "First come first served" (a subtle reference to my condition, because I have known all along what this Dr. Eardly thinks of me).

"Tell me what you have been doing this morning?"

I mustn't panic. Start from here. From where I am sitting now. The snow outside. The room. This table edge, which I am holding with both hands.

"Take your time thinking about it."

"Nothing special," I say. "Same as usual. Get up, wash, dress, shave, drink coffee, eat breakfast."

"Chicken?"

"Chicken? No, just the usual slice of toast and marmalade, from that yellow jar with the black lid, you know."

"You ate half a cold chicken from the refrigerator. A can of liver pâté, a couple of pineapple rings and a box of cookies."

"I am finding this a painful account. In broad outline I cannot agree with it."

"Who are you talking to?"

"Vera," I say, quickly, and panting slightly. "Listen carefully to me. I don't hurt a fly. I went for a walk this morning, with Robert. Down the path. In the Stevens' yard there was a pick-up truck from Salem. A red one without wheels. You can go and look for yourself. The usual junk. I didn't see Pat. Robert was chasing after some crows. We went to the beach. Into the wind. The white scent was all around me. But I thought about that only because other people always talk about the salty sea air. Even Pop does, he always talks about the salty sea air, too."

"Your father died in 1956."

I pick up a book that is lying on the table between us and turn it over with a furious bang.

"Did you imagine I didn't know that? To sum up, as Bahr always says at the end of a meeting, I walked along the beach, a little way down Atlantic Road, and then back towards home. Wind at my back. Any other business?"

"You phoned the library."

"When I came home you were on the phone," I reply. "I could see you through the window. I tapped against the glass but you didn't hear me. I waved and when you finally saw me you dropped the phone from fright."

"It was Joan from the lending department."

"I don't want you to work there anymore," I say. "I want you to stay with me from now on, Vera. When I am alone everything goes wrong. I don't know why."

"I haven't worked there for ages, Maarten."

"Good," I say. "That's all right, then."

Her narrow head with the brown hair wobbles on her wrinkly neck and her eyes are suddenly so dull and sad that I get up to comfort her. The blood throbs in my temples and I put my hands on her shoulders.

"Not so hard," she says.

My hands are cold and numb. I withdraw them. I look at the palms and slowly let them drop limply by my sides.

"I know the feeling," I say, "as if it someone has locked you up inside your own house. That's the feeling. But there is always a way out, Vera, always."

It is very understandable that she has to cry now. I sit down again. "I am with you," I say. "Whatever happens, I am with you. We'll have to get used to the fact that our world has become smaller, that you see fewer and fewer people, that you are startled when the phone rings, that all the days look alike. But we have each other, Vera, don't forget that." And I stroke her hair softly. Let her cry it out. I understand.

A human being can look for a long time without seeing anything. Robert can look too, but he is unable to recognize the tea caddy and the cheese slicer. He looks without seeing is what I mean. Try it for yourself. You always drink coffee of a particular brand and when they don't have any in stock at the drugstore you take a different brand, a different can. When you want to make coffee the next day, you look everywhere for the can of coffee. The remembered image of the old can is so strong that it makes the new brand, right there in front of your nose on the kitchen shelf, invisible. To see something you must first be able to recognize it. Without memory you can merely look, and the world glides through you without leaving a trace. (I must remember this well, because it will enable me to explain a great deal to Vera.)

I am standing by the window in the back room, looking at two scrawny squirrels chasing each other up the trunk of a crooked birch tree. Look at those swaying grey plumes. Whoops? A little dance step would be in pace here...no...not pace ... step ... pace...in place! A leak. There is a small leak somewhere. Hampers the thinking process. That is the sort of thing Simic would have said, at one of those rare moments when he raised a point. Tall, thin, taciturn Karl Simic, as brittle as china, cautious, timid, looking warily out of his dark, slightly squinting eyes. Dampens the thinking process. Simic used to play the piano rather well. The whole of Ravel's *Bolero*. Out of his head. Even though he was drunk. A song about a ship with so many guns. He sang the words to it, in German, his eyes raised to the ceiling. I only ever went to his house once. On the occasion of his forty-fifth birthday. Neither chick nor child did he have. After a few whiskies in that bar in Boston he invited me home. He lit only one small reading lamp. In the half-dark he told me a story of how his wife or girlfriend had deceived him with his best friend, that he had found a letter which left him in no doubt, how he had gone out and bought a bottle of bourbon and had drunk it all with that friend while they argued about the literary qualities of Hemingway's novels. In the end their disagreement ran so high that the friend had shouted: Next time there is a war you won't survive the camps but I will.

Simic then muttered something and I had to bend forward to hear what he said. He shouldn't have said that, he whispered. He shouldn't have said that. Why not? I asked. Because it's the truth, he replied.

We didn't drink bourbon that night, but vodka on the rocks. In the end Karl was so drunk that I had to lay him on his bed. He weighed little more than a child. He went on singing. Sombre Slav songs of which I didn't understand a word. There were lots of books in his bedroom. And a large painting of a ballet dancer floating in the air. I sat on the edge of the bed. Karl had finished singing. I was no longer quite sober myself. He was lying with his back toward me. I started telling him about Vera and about the only time I had been unfaithful to her. In Paris.

She sat down opposite me in an overcrowded restaurant that Leon Bahr had recommended to me. Fat and dark, she was wearing a shiny black silky blouse; there was something gypsy-like, something unbridled about her. It is difficult to avoid the eye of someone who is sitting across from you at a table.

I was eating *entrecôte au poivre.* She ordered the same. I took a *coupe dame blanche.* So did she. I was always one course ahead of her and watched how she ate, with tiny little bites, leaving nothing on her plate. I noticed how thin her fingers were only when she caught up with me at the coffee and cognac stage. She held her glass as if it were a baby's hand. She was slow and she was graceful. Unlike most fat people, she had not yet lost the power over her body.

We touched glasses very lightly and said our names. Maarten, Sylvie. As if these were the names of the glasses. And that was true. Our names, our pasts, did not matter that evening. This ritual was repeated three more times. Soon we were the only ones left in the restaurant. In clumsy French I had explained to her why I was in Paris. She worked somewhere in an office, she told me. *Allons,* she motioned me, when she noticed the waiters and waitresses in their white aprons standing leaning against the bar watching us. *Allons.*

We went. She lived close by. She pressed the light button in the hall of the apartment building and suddenly walked quickly ahead of me on tapping heels. *Vite,* she said, it will go out after a minute. Apart from her name and her occupation, that was all she told me that night, in a curiously light, almost girlish voice. For the rest, she made soft, contented, grunting sounds, deep down in her throat.

It was an event that happened to me but which I also wanted.

It was complete. Maybe because we had no past for each other nor wanted to acquire one. We moved in and over and out of each other. Pure lust, it was. Pure and anonymous. Finally she turned her enormous back with the imprints of my teeth in her left shoulder blade towards me and fell asleep. I got up, dressed, and vanished from her life. Outside, the dawn glimmered. Blackbirds sang. Only when the night porter at the Ambassador Hotel said my name did I remember who I was.

Had Karl heard what I said? He, too, was lying with his back to me. He said nothing in reply. I got up and left.

The next day he did not come to work. Nor the following days. Bahr drove to his house in person. The police did the rest.

We all attended his funeral. It was a beautiful cemetery, near Shipman's Wreck, a hilly area with tall oak trees. Bahr made a speech. He spoke of integrity, and that we would miss him. There was nothing in his words to suggest that Karl had cut his wrists in the bath and had drowned afterwards, as the autopsy showed.

No one mentioned him again. I often thought of that evening before his death. With a little less to drink we might have become friends then, I might have helped him overcome his shame, his shame at being alive while others were dead. Maybe.

No, that story about pure lust must have eluded him. He was asleep. Thinking of that evening I still see his back moving in tranquil sleep.

"Come," says Vera. "Come and sit down, Maarten."

Before her on the table lies an open photo album. "Dr. Eardly recommended this. A way of putting your memories in order," she says, sitting down beside me, turning a thick black page covered in photographs, while I stare in silence at the pictures with their scalloped edges.

I recognize the ripple of the wind in a pond, poppies flowering by a roadside, clouds above the sea with dark, frayed, stormy linings, the cropped grass of a lawn with a group of people on it in light, summery clothes, their arms around one another's shoulders. And smiling, of course, always smiling, as if life in the past was one long happy party. When photography was still something special and a print relatively expensive, everyone smiled when having his photograph taken. As if the picture would then be worth more.

Vera puts her forefinger on male and female figures and mentions names. Kitty, Janet, John, Fred. Three years ago, in Rockport.

I remain silent.

"You should concentrate more," she says. "You know it all, but you must try harder." She taps briefly with a gleamingly lacquered nail against my forehead.

I pull the album towards me and turn the pages back. Then it is as if a mist clears.

"Look," I say. "This was the boat elevator at the Postjesweg. Other people called it a ferry, but it wasn't, it was an elevator. The market gardeners from the Sloterpolder used to assemble here with their punts and flat-bottoms to go to the market. One by one the boats entered a kind of steel trough. Then the big cog-wheels overhead began to turn and each boat was lifted by thick cables into the Kostverlorenkade, swaying and trembling. Sometimes as many as forty boats were waiting, beside and behind one another, laden with vegetables and fruit in those flat crates they used to have."

"And this was taken from the window at home. Where you see all those green-houses and wooden shacks another world began, a water world full of punts, flat-bottoms, rafts and white foot bridges across the ditches. In the winter you could skate there endlessly. Frisian runners. Can you feel them still, pinching your feet, with those tight, brightly colored straps and those stiff leather heels?"

I look at Vera. She nods. "I remember it all," she says. "I went there with you often enough." I am so happy to hear her say this that I want to go on talking, without the photographs.

"At the beginning of the war you could still sometimes get stuff from the market gardeners in the *polder,* but in the last two years they had become price conscious. The heirlooms some people took there, in return for a head of lettuce or a few bunches of carrots!"

"You were lucky to have a job," she says.

That is true. People working in the municipal buying department were closer to the fire. You knew when something or other arrived by barge. Then it was sometimes possible to fix things before distribution began. Of course it wasn't right, but everyone did it. In a way we were all of us petty crooks in those days, and the crazy thing was that it suited everybody perfectly. It brought a lot of suspense and excitement into people's lives.

"Do you ever think of those days now?" I ask.

"Rarely," she says.

"It's things from the war I remember best," I say. "They're sharp, as if everything was standing still then, as if nothing moved."

"Yes," she says. "That's how I feel too. Days that never came to an end. Maybe it was partly because of the hunger. Hunger and cold."

"Pea soup!" We both say at the same time, that arch-Dutch concept. Pea soup. And it makes us laugh.

"Those bay windows were no good," I say. "After the war practically all of them had to be replaced. They jutted out too far, they caught too much wind, certainly in that storm we had that time."

"I had no idea it was so dangerous."

"Peas," I say, "I'd managed to get hold of half a pillowcase full."

"We were as happy as kings. I was so nervous, as if I was cooking dinner for the first time, I was so scared I might spoil something."

"Fred had crawled under the table, the wind was making such a din. It roared in all the chinks and cracks."

"It was lucky he'd crawled out of harm's way when it happened."

"I can see you now," I say. "Your hair flying in all directions because of the wind suddenly crashing in, and that plate of soup in front of you, suddenly full of splinters."

"A miracle we weren't hurt ourselves," she says.

"I was furious. Especially because I couldn't blame it on the Huns."

"We put the soup through the sieve, but we daren't take the risk."

"You were about to," I say, "you were standing in the kitchen straining the soup. You slowly and carefully poured it into a funnel over a sieve you had put on top of the saucepan. You cried when I said you had to throw the soup away."

"Such things you never forget."

"No," I say, "such things stay with you for ever."

She turns a few more pages. "Here," she says, "in the tea garden, do you remember? The camera moved because I was scared Fred would fall from that branch."

I nod. I see myself, about thirty-five years old. I am wearing a sweater with a dark horizontal stripe and shapeless grey pants. With a half-blurred face I look up at a child that sits astride a stripped branch. I nod again. I would love to know.

"Usually you took the photos," she says. "That's why there are so few of you."

"I wasn't much of a photographer, though. And I often forgot to take the film out and take it to the store."

"Do you remember that time we were given the wrong ones? Quite by chance I knew those people. I saw the woman occasionally at the grocery store, at De Gruyter's, that clean, tiled store where it always smelled so deliciously of roasted coffee which they ground for you in a big round grinder with a silver funnel on top."

"I know," I say, "but I can't remember what was in those photos."

"Neither can I, except that they weren't our vacation snapshots. We'd been to the Veluwe. Kitty wasn't born yet."

"And ours? Did we ever get those back?"

"No. I gave the others to that woman. The grocer knew where she lived."

"This one is in the wrong place, it should be much further back. We were only just married, everything is new, you see? We were so proud of our home. In those days it was all very modern, with those tubular steel chairs and that stern oak dresser with red lacquered doors."

"Pop's desk," I say, pointing at another photograph. She nods.

"And now it stands here," she says. "On the other side of the world. I wanted to sell it, but you insisted it had to come. Why was that?"

I look at the desk. "Some pieces of furniture from your childhood remain important to you in some way. You feel a kind of link with them, it's hard to say exactly why. I remember I was allowed to draw at it on Sundays. A white sheet of paper on a baize-green blotter full of inkstains and little marks of letters Pop had blotted. If you looked at them for a long time you could see all sorts of shapes in them, animals, faces. I used to copy them."

She turned the pages. These have captions, that makes looking at them a lot safer.

"Winterswijk, 1952," I read aloud. "What shabby clothes those children are wearing."

"There wasn't anything else. They weren't that cheap, actually. Fred had just recovered from pneumonia, that's why he looks so thin. And Kitty became sick two days later. Scarlet fever. I spent most of the vacation indoors in the boarding house. You went for lots of walks. First on your own and later with your mother who came down for a week."

"That can't have been much fun."

"Oh, yes, it was. It was the first time she really accepted me. Ever since that week I got on well with her. Look, here she is standing in the garden at the boarding house. Heaven, yes, 'The Turning-point', it was called."

Don't panic. After all, she remembers everything. So this is my mother. If I want to know anything about the past I can always ask her. "Mother" I say, and I look at the bespectacled woman who leans with broad hands on a white garden gate. "There probably was no better mother. She looked after me so well that I hardly remember a moment's quarrelling. When she was angry with me she merely remained silent. She would sit by the table with a cup of tea in front of her and look at me in silence with her brown eyes while with one hand she twirled a strand of hair that had come loose from her bun. I used to think that was much worse than having an argument, like I sometimes had with Pop. That accusing silence of hers, those fingers mechanically playing with that lock of hair. Inaccessible in her silent sadness, she was, as she sat by the table."

"She only wanted to protect you, that's all. She told me so later. You were a clumsy child, you used to fall off everything. You were always covered in scratches and bruises."

I nod and look at the greying lady in a spotted summer dress with puffed sleeves in front of the "The Turning-point" boarding house. Then I turn the page. "Goodness, Paris," I say, pointing at a color photograph of a wide boulevard lined with busy terraces.

"You took that one when you were in Paris for IMCO. Your hotel was over there, across the road."

Hôtel Ambassador, it says in thick white curly letters on a wall under a grey stone balcony.

"Hotels," I say scornfully, "they seem designed in order to be forgotten."

Strange how after a certain page—October 1956—the past suddenly springs into color. But even the colors do not help me. Maybe it is because of the photographs themselves. A camera makes no distinction between important and unimportant, foreground or background. And at this moment I myself seem like a camera. I register, but nothing or nobody comes closer, jumps forward; no one touches me from the past with a gesture, a surprised expression, and these buildings, streets and squares exist in towns and cities where I have never been and shall never go. And the closer the photographs approach the present, as appears from the dates written underneath, the more impenetrable and enigmatic they seem to become.

Vera points, Vera supplies the commentary. I nod. But I see that she can read in my eyes that her words clarify nothing.

Outside a horn is sounded. Vera gets up. "That must be Roberts from the hardware store."

"What is he coming here for?"

"The laundry-room lock is broken. The door won't shut. I'll show him where it is."

I stay behind, in front of the open album. A moment later I hear hammering and then the sound of a saw moving through wood with quick, expert pulls.

It is a good thing that doors which have been forced open can be repaired again. I have two left hands, but Vera keeps a close eye on any household deterioration. Not a plug gets broken but she has already bought a new one. A few weeks ago she had the children's room redecorated. It was a funny sight, Kitty standing up in the metal cot in the middle of the room. She was scared to go to sleep so far from the wall, she said. I had to read her a bedtime story. Fairy tales. Once upon a time. And suddenly I remember.

Quickly I turn the pages back. There is the photograph Vera showed me a minute ago. Kitty and Johan, her husband, and my son Fred. Vera and I had been married for forty years and that was why they both came over. This here is Janet, the eldest of the Cheevers' children further up the road. She has moved now. Kiss, their Pomeranian, is in it, too. He's dead. Run over by a tourist. When Kitty and Fred left, Vera and I both had a hard time of it. We both felt the same, although we didn't mention it to each other. It was possible that we would never see them again. That was in both our minds, we could tell from each other's face. But we kept silent about it.

When Vera enters I rub my hands and tap on the photograph. I talk so fast that I stumble over my words. With her purse in her hands she listens to me. I love her face when it laughs in that carefree way and little wrinkles of mirth appear in it, especially around her nostrils and mouth. I want to talk about our wedding photographs but I can't find them quickly enough. I would like to see that moment again when we stood, a little apprehensive and uncertain, before the registrar of marriages, while behind our backs sat numerous aunts, who never missed a family wedding, particularly when it was whispered that the bride was expecting, and who searched their purses for handkerchiefs when Vera said yes in a loud clear voice, as you can tell from the photograph. Her half-open mouth with the snowy-white teeth, the aunts dabbing away a tear here and there. I was so hoarse I had to clear my throat twice before I could answer the registrar's question. And then the wedding reception at her parent's house in Alkmaar, her jovial father who took us to a wooden seaside hotel in Egmond where we had to show our brand new marriage certificate, we looked so young, and indeed we were, I in a suit from the "Nieuw Engeland" boys' department.

Perhaps those photographs are in a different album. A festive feeling comes over me. I wouldn't mind a glass of beer.

I go to the kitchen and look in the refrigerator. Maybe Vera hasn't been out shopping yet. Shall I ask her to get a six-pack? Miller, that's the beer I like best here. Heineken is better, of course, but far too expensive. They drink that here as though it were champagne. The green label was always like a signal from home when I used to have lunch at Crick's. There was always some at one table or another. I ask Vera if there is any beer in the house.

"Why do you want beer all of a sudden?" she says. "Anyway, I'd want to ask Dr. Eardly first. Alcohol and medicine don't usually go together."

I don't quite understand what she is talking about, but I do not want to spoil the atmosphere now.

"The door has been mended," she says, and puts her purse on the piano.

Yet another riddle. Better not ask any further. I nod. She looks at her watch. "Why don't you lie down for a while?" she says. "Dr. Eardly said . . ."

"What have I to do with Dr. Eardly?"

"You don't actually need to go to sleep. You could play the piano." She looks at me somewhat anxiously and her voice trembles in spite of her determined tone.

I don't want to be a nuisance, so I get up and go to the piano. I pick up her purse and open it. She will have to pay Greta before long, and she has nothing but American money. But who would refuse dollars? No one. Greta's boyfriend is a prole, Pop says. He doesn't like her because she smells of perfume, which creeps into my shirt collar at which I sniff furtively in my room after the lesson. I am in love with Greta, but on no account is she allowed to know that. She might not want to give me lessons any more. It is for her that I practice. I don't care about Mozart and Bach. Only about that one little hour a week, alone with Greta, side by side at the piano, wrapped in a cloud of daffodil scent.

"Why are you standing by the piano like that?"

Vera's voice. She takes me by the arm. I must go and rest, she says. Only for an hour. No need to get undressed. Just lie down on the bed.

I enter the bedroom and grin. I chuckle softly to myself and start humming as if automatically. Greta's boyfriend is a prole.

When I wake up it is so dark I can't even see the church tower behind the Sweelinckstraat. All around the open belfry runs a wooden balustrade. Grandpa told me that someone jumped off it once. In this room I often dream of that. Or of shooting stars, which Pop sometimes points out to me in the evening sky. Shooting stars that burn up when they enter the earth's atmosphere. Maybe Grandpa will teach me how to play checkers tonight. He promised. I'll lie still until he calls me. I hear him playing his recorder at the back of the house. He also has a piano but it has such a heavy touch that I always make mistakes when he asks me to play something. He is playing long drawn-out notes ending in trills. It must be after five. Grandpa always plays from five till half past. Then he has his drink and exactly at six o'clock we start our supper.

"What time is it?" I ask Vera when she enters the bedroom and switches on the light.

"Quarter past five."

I nod contentedly and sit up on the edge of the bed. She pulls my tie straight. "Dr. Eardly is here."

Slightly stiff from lying on the bed, I walk to the open living-room door in the direction of flute music. Vivaldi by the sound of it.

A man in a navy-blue pants and a wasp-yellow sweater gets up from the settee surprisingly quickly when I enter. Vera switches off the radio.

"Hello, Mr. Klein," he says. A lot of gold in the corners of his mouth. He can't be older than forty-five. He enquires how I am, in the hearty, quasi-spontaneous tone in which all Americans address strangers. I nod, and pause in the middle of the room.

"Sit down, please, Maarten," says Vera, but the man makes a gesture as if to say he doesn't care. Then I sit down and he immediately drops down with a thud beside me in the settee and grabs hold of my wrist. Vera does nothing about it. She sits beside us on the two-seater, her hands clasped in her lap, looking at us, frightened and curious at the same time. The man smells penetratingly of aftershave.

"Been to Lorenzo the barber's, have you?"

"How did you guess?" he says, and wants me to straighten my right knee. He taps on it with a little swivel hammer that he has taken from a leather case. The lower leg jumps up. "Excellent," he says.

"Naturally," I say. "There's nothing wrong with me."

The man glances briefly in Vera's direction, a questioning look in his eye.

"I talked about it with him," she says. "We've been looking at old photographs together."

"A useful and agreeable therapy," says the man, and puts one leg across the other. No, he doesn't want to drink anything. Not even a Miller? Vera gives a startled look, but when the man shakes his head her face becomes calm again. People's facial expressions sometimes flash by so fast that I have no time to ascribe a meaning to them. Maybe they don't have a meaning. Maybe they are like the moving patches of sunlight among the trees in a forest.

"And how did it go?"

He seems to think I am crazy. The tone they usually adopt here when they address someone over sixty. Amiable condescention mingled with distaste. Never mind, let it pass.

"Seeing photographs is quite different from looking at photographs," I say. "Anyone can look at photographs, but seeing a photograph means being able to read it. On the one hand you have people and their cultural products, on the other hand nature. Trees, lakes, clouded skies speak a universal language in photographs that can be understood by anyone. Outside time, as it were. By contrast, people, buildings, roads, coffee cans and the like can be read only in a specific context, in time. You can't read that photo album on the table for the most part because you lack the necessary background information. You weren't there. In other words, you cannot form any further pictures about what is in there, because you cannot remember what could once be actually seen. It isn't your past."

I glow with effort. He is clearly finding it so interesting that he takes his diary and starts writing something. When I stop talking in order to give him a chance to write his notes, he says, "Please carry on."

Vera also seems to hang on my lips. But now that I have stopped, no more will come.

"Philip sends his regards to you—Philip, the bookseller," says the man, putting a notebook into his inside pocket.

"Oh, him. I haven't seen him for ages."

"You went there only the other day. You bought *Our Man in Havana* from him. A very good Graham Greene. Made into a movie as well. Who played the main part again?"

I shrugged my shoulders. Then Vera whispers a name, "Alec Guinness." Damn, she's right. This fellow does look like Alec Guinness. Let's hope he didn't hear her, because it may not be much of a compliment. Same jowls and broad ear-rims. I have to make an effort not to start chuckling.

"Maybe I did," I resume the thread. "When you don't have to go anywhere any more you just walk as you please. There's no harm in it. It can't go wrong. It's not all that good either, but be that as it may . . ."

He nods and suddenly gets up. He gives me a cool, dry hand. I wonder if he plays the piano? He has the hands for it. When I am about to ask him, he has already turned his back on me and is following Vera into the hall.

Peace and quiet, keep indoors, familiar surroundings, carry on with the therapy, I hear a man's voice say. And Vera's timid voice in reply: "Sometimes he's like a stranger to me. I can't reach him. It's a terrible, helpless feeling. He hears me but at such times I don't think he understands me. He behaves as if he were on his own."

I know exactly what she means. Like it was just then, when it all went wrong. All of a sudden I had to translate everything into English first, before I could say it. Only the forms of sentences came out, fragments, the contents had completely slipped away.

Furiously I glare into the front room. I seem to lose words like another person loses blood. And then suddenly I feel terribly frightened again. The presence of everything! Every object seems to be heavier and more solid than it should be (perhaps because for a fraction of a second I no longer know its name). I quickly lie down on the settee and close my eyes. A kind of seasickness in my mind, it seems. Under this life stirs another life in which all times, names and places whirl about topsy-turvy and in which I no longer exist as a person.

"Curious," I say to Vera as she enters the room. "Sometimes I just have to lie down for a moment. I never used to."

"It doesn't matter. Your time is your own." She sits down, picks up a book.

"Your time is your own." I repeat the phrase because it appears strange to me.

She turns the pages but isn't reading. I can tell from the look in her eyes that she doesn't understand me.

"It should be: you have time to yourself. That describes the situation better."

"Is that how you feel?"

"Less and less right."

"What do you mean?"

"Like a ship," I say, "a ship, a sailing vessel that is becalmed. And then suddenly there is a breeze, I am sailing again. Then the world has a hold on me again and I can move along with it."

"I find it so hard to imagine, Maarten. I can't see anything wrong with you at all. It is as if you were looking at something, at something that I can't see. Are you afraid at those moments? What exactly happens to you then?"

"I don't know. I can't remember. Only that feeling of a sudden heaviness, as if I am sinking through everything and there is nothing to hold on to."

"Dr. Eardly says it will be all right again, if you rest."

"Do you know what I sometimes think, Vera? Why do I have so few memories from my childhood? I think a happy childhood leaves few memories. Happiness is a condition, like pain. When it's gone it's gone. Without a trace."

"But there are other things that you remember perfectly. You remember everything about the elevator at the Postjesweg. I had forgotten all about that until you started talkiing about it."

I nod. A small engineering miracle. It was a machine but its wheels and cogs worked so slowly that it looked as though the vegetable boats were being lifted trembling and swaying from the depths by some magic force. I often wave from the bridge at the market gardener sitting in the poop and sometimes he waves back with his cap or wooly hat.

"Who are you waving at?"

I look at my raised right hand and quickly drop it. Reality comes to my aid in the shape of a black car that stops behind Vera's Datsun in front of the house.

"Dr. Eardly, that must be Dr. Eardly," I say quickly.

Vera gets up, puts the book she was holding in her hand upside down on her chair and goes to the door. I can read the title. *Our Man in Havana*. Rings a bell. I probably read it long ago, though I haven't the faintest idea what it is about.

"Hi, William," I say as the eldest Cheever boy follows Vera into the kitchen carrying a carton full of purchases.

William nods. He is tall, broad and shy, in his padded blue parka and jeans. And, of course, those running shoes that every boy around here ruins his feet in these days. A good lad, but you have to chat with him a bit before he loosens down . . . up!

I use words the wrong way around occasionally, I notice, very occasionally. Maybe I have suffered a very slight stroke. That can happen in your sleep, you don't need to have noticed it at the time. I have read about it somewhere. But as long as you're still conscious of everything it doesn't matter, does it?

I go to the kitchen and ask William how Kiss is, their white Pomeranian. It seems the question is not well received. Vera and William, side by side behind the kitchen table with the red-dotted plastic cloth, remain silent for a moment. Embarrassed like two children. Then Vera says to William: "Maarten's jokes are a bit gloomy sometimes. Don't take too much notice." William nods emphatically, with relief. The acne has left deep pits in his cheeks.

"Well, I'll be off, then," he says.

"Don't you want a beer?" I ask.

Behind William's back Vera motions no with her hands. Why? Why shouldn't the lad have a beer?

"No time," says William.

"Many thanks," says Vera.

"No trouble, Mrs. Klein," says William in reply.

How beautiful is this speaking from person to person, one after the other, like beads on a string.

I sit down at the kitchen table and watch Vera unpacking the purchases and putting them away in the kitchen cupboard. Sugar here, tea a shelf lower down. Every household has its own rules. That is why you often can't find your way around in someone else's kitchen.

"Sometimes," I say, "when you can't get the usual brand and you've bought a different can you don't even see the new one at first. The memory of the familiar can makes the new one invisible."

"I don't know what you're talking about."

"About coffee," I say, "cans of coffee."

When she has finished tidying up she pushes the empty carton under the kitchen table with one foot and asks me if I would like a bowl of soup. Oxtail soup.

"All right," I say.

She passes me the newspaper but I push it away again at once. Most of it is the same every day, anyway.

Stirring the saucepan of soup she says, "Why don't you go and lie on the settee and read the paper? I don't like being watched when I'm busy in the kitchen"

I put the paper over the book on Vera's chair and close the curtains. Then I switch on the television. I listen while looking at the stylishly groomed women and men of NBC news, busily gesticulating behind their desk. I understand everything they say. I can follow everything. Yes, it must have been a slight stroke, a very slight one. I won't tell Vera, she would only worry.

The food is very thin this evening, but I am not hungry, anyway. Beside my plate lies a green capsule. Vera says I must take it. It calms you down, she says.

"But I am already calm."

"Even calmer."

I hold the pill between thumb and forefinger and put it in my mouth and take a spoonful of soup.

"Oxtail soup," I say. "Nice."

"Your favorite soup," she says.

From the settee we watch the television. A documentary about the rise of Hitler. The familiar scenes of flags and banners and crowds of people, hysterically cheering the moustached little man on the balcony.

I was twenty-one then. I was engaged to Karen and no one in my family except Uncle Karel at the Twentse Bank believed there would ever be a war. Certainly not in the Netherlands. Karen. Would she still be alive? She was the first girl I ever saw naked, in her parents' cottage in Spierdijk. With her arms crossed above her head she pulled off her lemon-colored summer dress in one movement. She wasn't wearing a bra underneath. She sat down on the edge of the bed, tilted her white buttocks and pushed her even whiter panties down over her knees. She kicked them off her foot and held out her arms to me. Stark naked, I said jokingly, but I trembled like a reed and did not really know what to do. What I wanted to do at the moment was kneel before her. I had not been brought up religiously but that was what I wanted to do, kneel down to that naked girl with her blonde hair, one strand of which fell between her small pointed breasts. She helped me, but as soon as I felt her pubic hair against my belly I came, from sheer excitement. Leaning on her elbows she looked with a contented smile at the glistening white puddle on her tummy. Never mind, she said. You'll take longer in a minute. Later she told me she had had an affair with a married man, a teacher at school. She never realized how much I adored her. Maybe it was my own fault. I was very shy. Dad always made jokes about it. I'm sure that boy is going to be an archaeologist when he grows up, he said. All he ever looks at is the ground.

"What's the name again of that fellow with the dog's face and those little spectacles?" asks Vera.

"Himmler," I say. "Do you want to go on watching?"

"No, always that war. Might as well turn if off."

The picture leaps backward and vanishes into a white dot that continues to glow for a moment on my retina. Himmler, Hitler. I, too, lived through that war. It now seems inconceivable. But even front-line soldiers usually have only a vague idea of the campaign in which they have taken part.

"Do you know what I sometimes wonder?" I say. "Whether inquisitive extroverted people have more memories in later life than shy introverts."

"I wouldn't have thought it had much to do with it," says Vera.

"I used to be so shy my father called me the archaeologist, because I was always looking at the ground."

"When I first met you that didn't seem to be the case."

"I learned to play my part," I say. "But in reality I am still a shy person."

She looks at me with her emerald eyes above the wrinkly pouches of skin. I feel like a baby looking up at the face of his mother. My smile arises in the same way—all by itself—for no other reason than the recognition of the familiar face. I kiss her carefully on the cheek, but my lips slide away to her ear. Tears spring to my eyes.

"Stop it, you're tickling me."

"I would like to kneel in front of you," I whisper.

"Don't talk such nonsense," she says, gently pulling my hair. "Come on, silly," she says. "Let's go to bed."

While she gets undressed in the bedroom, I switch off the standard lamp in the living room. I pause in the doorway and look at the furniture. It has nothing to say to me. That is good. Tomorrow it will still be there in the same position. And the day after. That is good. I switch off the light.

"We're going for a walk, Robert," I say. "Just finish my coffee."

"Maarten, the doctor says you're not to go out. Here you are." Vera pushes a bowl of yoghurt and cornflakes in front of me.

"Since when does a doctor decide where I go or do not go? I'm not sick. At least I don't feel sick."

"You're a little confused. You might get lost."

"Get lost?"

"Yes, because you sometimes forget which way to go."

"Not when Robert is there. He knows the way home, no matter where he is, even from the center of Boston."

"The other day you lost Robert when you were out."

I remain silent.

"Finish your yoghurt."

Clearly, she is inventing stories to test me. If I confirmed them I would be lost. I would lose myself in her fabrications. Maybe that doctor of hers told her to do it. Try to find out if he can still distinguish reality from fiction. A test. Better not reply. Better not respond to anything. I must retain my hold on ordinary life. To think that this should ever have become my ideal, holding on to the ordinary routine of events. At moments when I can no longer do that, I must try to imitate this routine of events. And if even that should fail, only then would I have to start inventing life itself (but not her).

Yes, I long for the pleasure of the daily routine, the course from one event to the next. It is necessary to fill your life. But I can still use language. I remember clearly the first time I told my mother a lie. The amazement that my words were believed even though they said things that were not true. That the difference could not be noticed! I was five, maybe six. I was late getting home. I said the bridge had stayed open "a very long time because two barges had bumped into each other" (while in fact I had stayed out playing with a friend). Yes, that lie was a tremendous discovery. My father and mother nodded. So beside the visible and verifiable reality there were many others, apparently indistinguishable from the real one.

If need be—if I really have to—I shall invent a life for myself from minute to minute and believe in it, like my father and mother believed that story about the two barges bumping into each other, one of which "had almost sunk."

"Where can the children be?" I say. "It's late enough."

Vera does not reply. She gets up.

"Or has the school bus gone past already?" I ask.

"Yes, Maarten," she says, "you were still asleep when the bus went past."

"Did I sleep as long as that?"

"It's because of the medicine. Dr. Eardly said it would make you sleep soundly and he was right. I had to wake you up."

"What time is it, then?"

"Past twelve."

She leaves the kitchen. Robert follows her.

"I'm coming, Robert."

I always feel a bit stiff in the mornings but that will soon go when I take my walk.

Have I gained that much weight recently? My coat is so tight. And why is the door locked? I tug at the door knob a couple of times. Maybe it is stuck or frozen.

"Come along, Robert!"

I wait for the dog and look at the coat stand. Hurriedly I take off Vera's wine-colored coat and correct my mistake before she catches me when she comes out of the laundry room.

"Have you seen Robert?"

"He's outside."

"I'll be off, then."

She posts herself with her back against the front door.

"The doctor says you mustn't."

"I'm not sick. There's nothing wrong with me. Robert," I call out, "Robert, come here!"

"He'll come back of his own accord."

"Am I never allowed out again, then?"

"Not now."

"But I want to go fishing. I made a date with Gerard and Klaas," I lie to her. "Go on, let me."

"Come along to the kitchen. You haven't finished your food."

"At school they say too much dairy produce is bad for your teeth." (But what can you do? Once I am out of the house I can do what I like.)

I sit down by my plate of porridge and chew demonstratively. In a minute she's bound to say: Don't dawdle so over your food.

"Has Pop gone to work yet?"

"Maarten, it's me, Vera!"

"Don't shout at me."

She hides her face in her hands. Why is she so upset all of a sudden? Why is she crying so heartrendingly?

"Don't cry. I don't want you to cry."

"Vera," she sobs, "I'm Vera!"

"Of course you're Vera," I say, "did you think I didn't know?"

She suddenly get up. "I'm just going to drop in on Ellen Robbins," she says. "I'll be back in a moment. You do the crossword meanwhile."

Strange that she didn't tell me she was going out. Maybe she has gone shopping. I quite like being at home on my own, so I can secretly peep in Pop's desk. On Sundays he lets me draw at it. A white sheet of paper on a baize-green blotter covered with inkstains and the marks left by Pop's blotted letters. When you look for a long time you see all kinds of things in it—animals, faces.

The door of the little cupboard inside the desk, behind which there are three deep drawers filled with papers, is locked, but I have the key in my pocket. I pull out the middle drawer and grope with one hand among his papers. I hold a letter in my hand, part of a letter, for there is no beginning, it starts somewhere in the middle.

In the afternoon I was free and I went for a walk in the Latin Quarter. It was pleasant weather for strolling along the galleries and second-hand bookstores. My fingers itched but my French isn't good enough for reading. I bought a few antique postcards of Paris which I enclose. Two more days and I shall be back with you. In spite of the delights of the *"ville lumière"* I miss you all every hour of the day (especially you) when seeing all these beautiful things. Kisses, Maarten.

I pull the drawer right out of the desk and turn it upside down, but no matter how I search and rummage among the papers, the rest of the letter does not emerge. Only piles of documents related to IMCO meetings, when the club was still housed in Bonn. I remember those five years in Bonn, from 1962 until 1967 to be precise. But Paris?

I sit down at the desk and reread the fragment. Without a doubt my handwriting.

"You've been to Paris," I say aloud, but the sentence does not help me. I might just as well have made it up, now, at this moment. If I cannot remember it, the words mean nothing. I fold the letter twice and slip it into my inside pocket. Outside, a dog is barking.

"Robert," I say, and get up from my desk and go to the window.

Barking, Robert dashes over the snow around the house, following me, but all the doors are locked. They have locked me in and left me on my own.

I stand in the back room and watch Robert nervously circling round an ash tree and jumping up against it so that the snow falls from the branches onto his back. This startles him so much that he comes darting towards me like an arrow and leaps up at the window, only to slide back, his claws scratching across the glass. He looks at me with his dark moist eyes full of sadness.

I have no choice. Otherwise he will die of cold. I pull a chair from under the table, take hold of the back with both hands, and push its legs through the glass, which falls out with a great clatter. A few more thrusts and the hole is large enough for Robert to jump through. I run my fingers briefly through his damp pelt. He sniffs at the heap of papers beside my desk and then lies down in front of the radiator as if nothing had happened.

I feel a bit cold. A cup of hot tea would do me good. I go to the kitchen and turn on the gas. The kettle, where is the kettle? "Kettle," I say, "kettle," but the thing is nowhere, not in any of the kitchen cupboards. Perhaps in the living room. Vera sometimes uses it to water the plants. Not there either. I open the store cupboard but no matter how I search behind plates and glasses, I cannot find a bar of chocolate anywhere. Nor are there any pear drops. Maybe she has gone to the store. I sit down at the piano and first press the damper pedal before I start. Grandpa is having his afternoon snooze upstairs so I must play very quietly. The keys move heavily and stiffly. Or is it that my fingers are too cold? Then I hear the front door open. "I'm in here, Grandma," I call out to her from beside the piano.

In a wine-red coat with large black bone buttons Vera rushes past me to the kitchen, sniffing loudly. Then she comes back and runs toward a broken window. She looks first at the shattered glass and then at me. "Jesus," I hear her mutter. Then she goes to the telephone. I sit down on the settee and fold my hands. Fear wells up in my stomach and then in my mouth. I swallow a few times and then I hear her talking to someone about a broken window pane. She doesn't say I did it and I appreciate that (although I cannot remember how that window came to get broken). How are you to feel guilty if you can't remember anything about an incident? If you see only the consequences without knowing the cause? You have to refuse. Otherwise there is no end to it and anyone could always blame you for everthing. And yet I feel guilty.

When she has finished her call she bends down and pulls papers together that are lying on the floor beside the desk. I can easily help her. I get up.

"Take your coat off first," I say.

"It's freezing cold in here."

She's right. I go to the hall and take my coat from the hook.

"Where are you off to?" she says in a very frightened, screechy voice when I enter the room with my coat over my arm. Calmly I put it on.

"Nowhere," I say, "I feel cold, that's all."

She pushes the drawer into the desk and sits down on the chair. "Maarten, what does all this mean?"

That is precisely the question. The meaning, the cause without which the consequences are senseless, inexplicable. In confusion, and perhaps also in order to gain time, I fumble in my inside pocket. I unfold the sheet of paper. Then I remember.

"The worst was that letter about Paris," I say, and start automatically walking around in circles. "I first thought it was a letter of Pop's but then it suddenly turned out be be my name at the end. And only then did I see it was also my handwriting. Only then. You look."

I hold up the paper between forefinger and thumb. "I can't remember how I have lived exactly, Vera," I whisper with my coat on in the middle of the room, holding up the letter in my hand like a piece of evidence (like a scene from a bad play, equally ridiculous).

"Don't take it to heart," I say therefore. "I'll remember in a minute."

"It was in 1963," she says.

"When we were living in Bonn," I say.

"You see, you do remember."

"Bonn, yes, but not Paris."

"I'll show you some photographs of it later. You were at an IMCO congress. Something about European interaction."

"Counteraction they probably mean. Eating and drinking and putting spokes in each other's wheels."

"That's what you said then, too."

"And I still think exactly the same," I say with determination.

"As long as they know. There's someone coming. Look, it's William. Where's Kiss? He hasn't brought Kiss with him."

"Maarten, will you remember once and for all: Kiss is dead. Has been for a long time. So please don't start about that dog again to William. I'm only too glad he's willing to help us with that broken window."

"William is a good lad. A bit quiet, but when you give him a beer or two he loosens up all right."

"We don't have any beer."

"Then I'll make tea. Oh, yes, by the way, have you seen the kettle anywhere?"

"I'll make the tea myself. Later."

"I couldn't find the kettle."

"It's where it always is, on the draining-board by the window."

While Vera opens the door I go to the kitchen. There stands the kettle. I must have looked right through it. It smells of gas in here. I check the burners but all four are off. Maybe there is a leak somewhere in the pipes. That is dangerous, an engineer will have to be called in. I go to the living room.

"Hi, William," I say. William is crouched in front of a broken window and carefully pulls a large pointed piece of glass out of the frame. "Nice of you to call on us. Haven't you brought Kiss with you?"

William does not reply. As usual. In a while we'll pour a few beers into him and then his tongue will loosen. You'll see.

"It is nice of William to help us with that broken window, isn't it, Maarten."

"Very decent of you, William," I say, and rub my hands together.

Vera goes to the kichen and returns with a brush and dustpan. Carefully, William sweeps the bits of glass into the pan. Some of the pieces are too big, they won't fit into it. I want to help him but he says it's too dangerous. The larger pieces he carries carefully out of the house between finger and thumb and puts them on the snowy flower bed, at the spot where in summer there grows a tall, untidy tuft of wild marguerites. Vera goes out into the hall. (What a lot of activity for this hour of the day. Pleasant to watch.)

"Maarten, where is the hammer?" she calls out from the hall.

"Where it always is. In the toolbox."

"It isn't there."

"Women and tools." Shaking my head I go the laundry room. On the shelf, to the far left. Hey, that's funny. Who could have removed the hammer from here? Just to make sure, I look inside the washing machine, but it isn't there. (Of course it isn't there!)

"I don't understand it at all," I say.

"What a nuisance," says Vera. "Now William can't nail that old door in front of it, the one that's still standing in the shed."

But William says he'll find another solution for it. He goes to the shed in the yard and comes back with an old, weathered door and a monkey wrench. Nails he has brought himself, in a gold-colored box with a convex lid that he takes from the pocket of his parka. A pretty little box. But William has no eye for pretty things. At any rate, he does not reply when I make a complimentary remark about the little box.

It is always disagreeable when someone doesn't answer you or pretends he hasn't heard you. That happens sometimes at meetings, too. The words remain in the air, as it were, and the person concerned tries his utmost to conceal his embarrassment and irritation by giving a sharp twist to his speech, addressing someone who just happens to be looking in his direction.

"At least, if you compare it with today's packaging," I therefore continue to Vera. "All plastic and cellophane. They would do better to use the money they spend on advertising to make attractive packaging."

Now William does answer. He is crouching with his back towards me, but he has obviously been listening.

"Packaging is packaging," he says. "You throw it out anyway."

"Except a little box like that," I say. "You yourself are using it for a different purpose now."

"It's Pop who does that," says William, and carries on hammering with his monkey wrench.

I fumble in my pocket and go to the desk, quick, lock the little door before he comes home and finds out that I have been rummaging around in his belongings. He'd be furious. Not even Mama ever touches those drawers. There, no one has noticed.

"I get you," I say, "Just call me Maarten. Why haven't you brought Kiss? Such a nice dog."

William raises his eyebrows, above his pale blue, somewhat helpless eyes. He looks towards Vera as if she might be able to answer my question. And she does answer it.

"You know what Kiss and Robert are like together."

"They tear each other to bits!" calls out William.

Why does he shout so and why does he suddenly make that relieved, almost farcical face? Sometimes people's facial expressions and the words they speak don't seem to tally quite, like in the cartoons in the Sunday paper, where the colors sometimes go outside the lines of the drawing.

William wipes his right hand on his jeans before shaking hands with me and Vera, and lets a shiny little brass box, which I wouldn't mind having myself, slide into his pocket. Nice of him to call in. He's a pleasant, friendly lad. A bit on the quiet side, but after a beer he loosens up sometimes. Vera follows him into the hall. She says I should take my coat off. What am I doing with my coat on indoors?

Grandpa used to have a whole lot of gold-colored tin cigar boxes in his shed at the bottom of the yard. He used to keep nails and screws in them. They had medals printed on them with the effigies of kings. Under each medal, in a curve of small black letters, was the name of a foreign city and date. There was a smell of oil in the shed. *Penetrating oil,* that is a expression he often used. *Penetrating oil,* rustles through my head, *penetrating oil,* again and again, *penetrating oil,* at the front of my mouth so that I have to swallow so as not to say to Vera, *penetrating oil,* who enters with a tray of rattling tea-cups and I ask: Where are the children, it's past four, pointing at the clock and staring at the hairline on her forehead and the tiny specks of pigment just below and feeling her hand holding mine as if she were trying to shake me awake, and still all the time those words, like a neon advertisement flickering up among the other words and although I no longer know which words, they are words, I can still hear the sound, see the outline, I can even still count the letters, two words which I cannot say, my mouth wide open, while she looks at me with that patient, loving, anxious look, as if I somehow no longer come up to the mark, an old horse they leave in the stable, and asks me if I want to do the crossword.

Shake my head resolutely!

"No more strange words! I want to think, in short clear sentences."

"What of?"

"I want to think, in short, clear sentences."

"Of the past?"

"The past?"

She takes my hand again. "You're tea is getting cold."

"I'm waiting for the children."

"Which children?"

I take a poor view of this conversation. As soon as I say something she seems to want to talk me into a trap. Look around. The interior. In the background fresh snowflakes flutter. I nod.

"My peepshow. With cotton wool instead of snow and dwarfs that I had cut out of a book of fairy tales and a tiger from my zoo box. Made of lead, on a base, with yellow and black stripes. A tiger in the snow and over the top a transparent sheet of red cellophane so that it looked as if the snow was on fire. For two cents, until the boys came, the big boys, and snatched the shoebox from my hands and knocked it flat against the rim of a garbage can."

"Don't cry, Maarten. It's a long time ago."

I rub my cheeks dry with the back of my hands. Where did those tears come from?

"Sometimes the thoughts move so fast that I hardly have time to think them, they wash through me and then I have to cry. And then suddenly everything stands still again, rigid as a magic-lantern picture and it is as if nothing will ever be able to move again and you have to start walking in order to get things going. Just walk and walk because otherwise you can no longer feel you belong anywhere, or that time passes."

"I wish I could help you. I would so much like to help you. Maarten, why can't our life remain as it was? Why does this have to happen?"

"My tea is cold."

"You forgot to drink it. Shall I make some more?"

"The children won't come now, anyway. It's much too late."

Robert gets up from beside the radiator and stretches himself with straightened front legs. He slowly comes towards me. Without knowing it, dogs have a built-in clock. They know exactly when they have to be let out. I briefly stroke his smooth back the wrong way. "You're right, Robert, it's time for our daily walk."

"You have already taken him out, Maarten."

Vera's face looks red and her lips are thin and tight under her sharp nose, suddenly the nose of an old woman, with a small white bloodless tip.

"Honestly, you've forgotten, but you have already let him out."

I look hesitantly at the dog, but it seems Vera is right this time, for Robert nestles down again in his old place by the radiator. So she must be right. Animals can't lie. "Aren't I forgetful."

"I love you the way you are," she says. "It doesn't matter."

I get up because suddenly, very suddenly, I have to pee. Hot stabs in my abdomen. Where do they suddenly come from? What is it that lurks inside my body and has it in for me?

I yawn, so loudly, my mouth so wide open, that it clicks in my ears. Try to pee in an orderly fashion now. At home you can clatter as you like, uninhibitedly, if need be with the door open.

I enter the room, push the bolt and switch on the light. Always try the bed with your clothes on first.

I lie on my back and look around me. This is a room with a so-called personal touch in the furnishings. I'm not too keen on that. As if just before your arrival somebody had lived in it who hurriedly grabbed his belongings together. And forget half of them in the process, I notice. Toothbrush, shaving cream. I'll collect it all together and take it down to the reception. No, give me a Holiday Inn or the Hilton any day. Close the door behind you and straight away the feeling: nobody knows where I am, nobody knows I exist. A mischievous feeling of freedom, or escape. That in principle, from now on, this anonymous, impersonal room, you could take a *totally different direction*. Not that you will do so, but the feeling in itself is enough to make you rub your hands contentedly and look at yourself in the mirror with satisfaction.

I undress, throw my clothes—as always when staying in a hotel—on the floor, and climb into bed. I leave the light on. I always do. Should there be a fire, every second matters. Make sure you get to the emergency exit before panic breaks out and people trample each other.

There is a knock on the door. Perhaps an urgent message, a telegram. "Just a minute!" I get up, pull my pants on and unlock the door.

"It's you, is it?" I say to Vera. "There's nothing wrong with the children is there?"

"Get dressed, quickly," she says. "The doctor is here."

Fear thumps in my throat. There must be something wrong with Fred again. How many times have I sat in the emergency room of some hospital or other with that boy?

In my agitation I can't manage my necktie. And there's no time for shoelaces either. I blink against all the light around me. A man sits on the two-seater, fairly young-looking. That must be the doctor. I walk towards him and half stumble, so that he rises hastily and just manages to stop me from falling. Shamefacedly I look at the laces that hang loosely over my shoes. "Please excuse me. I was in a hurry. I hope there's nothing seriously wrong with Fred?"

The smile on the doctor's face reassures me.

"There's nothing wrong at all, Mr. Klein. I've only come for a chat."

"Do you have time for that as a doctor?"

"I do these days. People in Gloucester aren't sick very often."

Gloucester? Gloucester? Yes, I see. Businesslike approach, Maarten. This man wants something from you. They always start amiably, just a touch too cordial. That gives them away at once. It always indicates ulterior motives. In such cases Simic's method must be employed. Simic explained it to me once after work. We were sitting in the cocktail lounge where Karl always went after work before taking the subway home. A smart, somewhat dark establishment divided into dark purple velvet-upholstered boxes with those chalice-shaped milky glass table lamps from the twenties. Simic, Karl Simic. A Yugoslav name, I believe. Pronounce: Simmitch. He used to go there and drink a couple of whiskies every day. Yes, he could hit the bottle at times, old Karl.

"Are you thirsty?" asks Vera. "You're smacking your lips so."

"Whisky on the rocks."

There's a man sitting in the room with a square, rustic face, baggy cheeks, large earlobes, and a rough, blond crewcut. He's there. He laughs. He knows nothing about Simic's method. On his lap lies a photo album of which he is turning the pages. He examines one particular photograph closely and then hands me the open album.

A wedding photograph of all things. I'm not in the mood for that at all. But Simic would say: Rule number one: repeat your interlocutor's words with a polite smile while nodding your head amiably in support. Gaining time is everything, especially at the beginning of a conversation.

"Is that a photograph of your wedding?" asks the man.

"Is that a photograph of your wedding?"

Look up at a slant, between the two of them, and keep nodding your head. Then I say six times in quick succession, "Yes." This is Simic's second rule: raise politeness to ritual heights. Even when you don't agree with anything, start by comfirming everything, but belie by frequent repetition the affirmative nature of your statements.

"Yesyesyesyesyesyes."

I put the album, *wham*, back on the settee. Must get up, walk around, and begin to gesticulate with my hands in anticipation of the words I feel coming.

"Let us try to tackle the problem first in general terms. They are people who are destined for each other, aren't they, hand in hand, he in black, she in white. But have you noticed those bystanders, those groups of people on the lawn? All of them potential candidates for this marriage! In other words: man pretends to himself he is *leading* a life, a meaningful existence. There is little to be said against this notion, although I must say it has no foundation, a mere illusion, shifting sands. If we look at it more globally, universally, we come to the conclusion that we are particles, female and male particles, moving around in society and sometimes accidentally meeting and fusing and then we talk of a marriage while all other possibilities continue to be present in the background. The erotic background chorus, Mr. . . . ."

"Doctor, Dr. Eardly."

"Look, Eardly, the temperature is rising. Two degrees or so. Before you know where you are, everything is in bud, the birds are twittering everywhere. The whole gigantic mating machine gets into motion again. Without visiting cards, name plates or address lists."

I pause in front of the open photo album. "Some of them are dead. Others are still alive. You can estimate it but you can't see it."

"What was your wedding day like? Do you remember what your wife looked like on that day?"

"May I ask you what is the meaning of this impertinent question?" I say, and walk out of the room without further ado. The last move in Simic's method. A slow, friendly opening, a moderate middle game and then an endgame that bags the loot quickly and aggressively. You simply leave for a leisurely pee and then re-enter the arena in which your opponent has been left in utter confusion.

A bit over the side, it runs across the floor. Jesus, that's bad, but I can't hold it now. Robert comes to my aid, he licks it up. A dog is ever a trusted friend. He looks at me briefly with his yellowish eyes, beside the stone jar in which the umbrellas are kept.

"Come, we're going for a little walk, Robert."

Then someone puts an arm around my shoulders from behind and pushes me into the room, in the direction of a piano (perhaps wants me to play something for him? Or do I have to practice?). I sit down and start playing Mozart's adagio, but he is standing beside me with a hypodermic syringe. Behind my back I hear someone crying, a woman.

"We know that from the war," I hiss, and knock the syringe out of his hand. The man bends to pick it up and I use the opportunity to sit down quickly at the table, opposite Vera.

"Don't cry," I say, "I'm in complete control of the situation."

I see how the man lets his syringe slide into a soft black leather doctor's bag.

"I am not a hero," I say, "but betray someone, never. The Nazis will lose the war, that is beyond question. The greater part of the country has already been liberated. The Queen has arrived in Eindhoven, they say. We must persevere, no matter how hungry we are."

The man is holding a soft leather bag in front of his stomach with both hands. Looks just like a doctor's bag. He is listening but I can tell he doesn't understand me. He looks at me almost timidly.

"It's war. People do the craziest things. In the long run you don't find anything crazy any longer. But only among ourselves, you mustn't talk about it outside, they're still prowling around, walls have ears. You can stay the night here. You're still in enemy territory, after all. It's dangerous outside. Shall I show you the guest room upstairs?"

"Just as you please. There are a few collaborators living near here, so it really is dangerous."

The American still does not react.

"What are you sitting there for, Vera? Get the man something to eat. Maybe he hasn't had any food for days."

"Nick," she says to the man, in a choking, imploring voice. He nods briefly in her direction, opens a black leather bag and takes out a hypodermic syringe. He disappears into the kitchen with it. I hear water running.

"Have we any food left? Or has it all gone?"

"Push up your sleeve," says Vera and unbuttons one of my shirt cuffs.

"I didn't realize I was in such a bad state," I said.

The mans enters the room and before I realize it the needle is in my arm.

"Liquid food," I mutter. "I was in bad need of it. I can feel it already. My stomach is filling up. Thank you, thank you both very much."

Wash . . . wash . . . wash . . . A woman is standing behind me. I can see her in the mirror. A chocolate-colored blouse printed with leaf-green French lilies, a black skirt. Her face doesn't go with the rest of her appearance, I think, it seems to be detached from it. She is holding a beige bath towel in her outstretched, trembling hand. Wash . . . wash . . . wash . . . wash.

"That's enough now, Maarten."

Turn around and take the towel from Vera. Rub. Nice, that rough towelling against your bare shoulders. Rub. And then I have lost the towel. She is holding it in her hands.

"Give it to me!"

"You must get dressed now, Maarten."

"I am not tired. As far as that is concerned you are right in what you say." (What a cumbersome manner of speaking.)

Skin that is beginning to feel thick and numb again. Can no longer feel the shirt (as if I am not really wearing it).

Behind me in the doorway stands a woman. Her brown hair falls in a lock towards the right across her forehead. Remarkably smooth cheeks in an otherwise old face that seems to move away ever further and comes closer again only after I have briefly looked away from the mirror to the wall beside it. She is keeping an eye on me. (Could she have been assigned to me? By whom?) Tie, where is my tie?

You should never try to put on your tie in front of the mirror. All that movement in reverse makes you dizzy. It confuses your fingers. Shut your eyes and do it by touch, let your fingers carry out the correct movements from memory. Suddenly I feel strange fingers at my neck. They fiddle with the stand-up collar of my shirt. (I am perfectly capable of doing it by myself.)

"I can do it, Mama."

"Don't call me Mama."

"What makes you say that, Vera?"

I turn, the sound of Vera's voice still in my ears. The little hollow in her neck is deep and sunken, almost black. How chic she looks today.

"Where are we going? We don't have to go to a birthday, do we? I hope we haven't forgotten Pop's birthday, like we did last year? That voice on the phone. I could have sunk through the floor in shame."

"Come along, now."

"Where are we going, Vera? Are we going out? You're all dressed up. Is it someone's birthday? If I've forgotten, you must tell me."

Ah, a room. Outside there is snow everywhere. I don't like the winter, I clench my fist against it. As I did when I was a little boy, against the lightning. I used to crawl under the living-room table and clench my right fist against the "heavenly force," as Pop, standing by the window, called it. I looked fearfully through the orange fringe of the tablecloth at the flashes of lightning and his dark figure, at each flash sharply outlined against the black blur of the window. I was scared, scared and yet longing to be struck.

"Come and sit down."

"Won't you give me a kiss? I must be off in a minute."

"You don't have to go anywhere. You're free."

"Did they phone from IMCO? Did Leon Bahr call?"

"He called to say you could stay at home, yes."

"No more meetings this week, I suppose. I'll get some wood from the shed."

"William Cheever has already stacked some in the laundry room. Enough for the whole week."

"Nice lad, that. Was Kiss here too? I didn't see him."

"No, he'd left Kiss at home. Stay where you are now, I'll get the coffee."

Of course, that is the smell I've been smelling all this time. It belongs to coffee. (Get up! Walk to the window!)

Two degrees above zero. We're moving in the right direction. There are already black thaw-holes in the snow. A little while longer and you'll hear the dripping of melting snow all day as if taps were running all over the house. But there's no way of telling. One year isn't like another. If you look at Pop's graphs you can see that at a glance. No question of any rule or regularity. Or perhaps there is, but we can't see it. A human being is too small for this life. What a delicious smell there is here. It is as if I have unexpectedly fallen into the day because of this smell. Or rather, as if the smell is inviting me to do so, with its sharp, scintillating message.

"Here comes the coffee-lady. We'll take a seat and enjoy the most delightful moment of the day. A lot of sugar, please."

"Maarten, one spoonful is enough."

"More, more. Come on, we only live once." (To tell the truth, it's more because of the stirring, an action which I could, how shall I put it . . . a whirlpool appears in the coffee when you stir fast, you stare and stare in the swirling black hollow inside the cup, which at the same time moves and is still.)

"Maarten, look what you're doing!"

"I bestir myself to stir."

How amusing, to burst into humor. (This must be where "bursting out laughing" comes from.) Well, what does it matter if you make a bit of a mess in your old age? No harm done. Now the sugar is at the bottom again. Slowly lift the sugar on the spoon. As careful as can be. Once they were beautiful, separate, white glistening grains and now look: what muck. Like the brown slushy snow in Field Road. Everything gets filthy. You must try to remain spotlessly clean yourself.

"Don't mess about with your coffee like that, or I'll take it away."

Nod. Yesyesyes. "Absolutely right. Approved and signed."

"Dear Maarten, will you listen."

"Dear Maarten, will you listen." Simic's method. Pronounce: Simmitch. Always works. Look how she is briefly knocked off balance. No, those Yugoslavs aren't so dumb by any means. Poor fellow. I have to swallow a couple of times to hold back my tears, grab the edge of the table and blink my eyes. How frayed this tablecloth is. In a moment Ellen and Jack Robbins will be here and we'll have this old rag on the table. I take hold of the frays and then it suddenly comes back to me just in time. Sometimes I can't get at a particular word, it lies hidden behind another word with a similar meaning. And a wrong word leads you to wrong thoughts and makes you do wrong things; words act like railroad points. These aren't called "frays" but a "fringe." Deliberately sewn on. (Belongs to the tablecloth, is part of it, stupid fool!)

Let's see if this coffee is still drinkable. It's rather nice like this, so sweet. There used to be cookies that were as sweet at this, they were long and coated with sugar. Ladyfingers!

Come, I ought to talk to that woman over there. She sits there so sadly behind her cup of coffee, as if she were all on her own in a snack bar. You see them sometimes in Boston. All alone among all those newly wiped, damply shiny Formica tables and chairs under a bare fluorescent tube, behind a tepid cup of weak coffee. What a way to start the day!

"Do you remember what ladyfingers looked like?"

She reacts strangely. At least I think so. Maybe she doesn't want to be spoken to. She gets up and turns on a radio somewhere. As long as it isn't that German braying, I don't mind. Fortunately, we are so remote here that we haven't had to hide our radio. The neighbors can be trusted here.

Music. Don't know it. A clever pianist, you can tell. I would need to practice for years to get that far. When you see all those black and white keys lying side by side and you listen and you know the music is hidden somewhere down there between the keys. And because you haven't practiced hard enough all those possibilities will be denied you. And that isn't all yet, by any means. All the music that is still to be made can be guessed there. You look at those black and white keys as if at any moment they might begin to move.

"Have you seen my practice book anywhere?"

She must have left the room. Surely it must be lying somewhere on the piano? If I don't practice this week I'll be in trouble with Greta and I don't want that. I think she is the most beautiful girl I know. If I dared I would very carefully lay my head in her lap, close my eyes and lie very still, feeling how she breathes, how she lives, bare, underneath that lemon-colored dress of hers.

"Here's your book. You asked for it, didn't you?"

"I think I have read this book before. Or have I only seen the movie based on it? Be that as it may . . . It doesn't matter. I don't remember the movie either, actually, if I ever did see it."

I pick up the book. Start reading. An echo rises from the sentences. As if I had seen this page before, as an image, in a flash. What do they call that feeling again, I read an article about it once. *Déjà vu*. A short-circuit between brain neurons. The image is registered a fraction of a second before the awareness of the image occurs, and so it seems you recognize something that you know for sure you can't ever have seen before.

"We're going to have company."

A sentence fired at me from nowhere. A sudden turn in the conversation that must be undone immediately.

"*Our Man in Havana,*" I say. "I think I have read this book before. Or am I confusing the book with the movie?"

"Maarten, we're going to have company. A lady will come to look after you. When I have to go out for a while . . . Go shopping and so on."

"Since when do I have to be looked after? I'm not a child, am I?"

"You've become so forgetful, Maarten. You keep forgetting what you are doing. It can be dangerous for you to be all alone in the house."

I cast a quick glance at her. She means what she says, I see fear in her slightly screwed-up eyes. Dangerous in the house, it echoes in my head. It confirms my idea that there is indeed something wrong about this house sometimes. As if shifts occur in the interior arrangements, as in an office with movable partitions.

"She'll look after your medicine, make sure you rest at the right times."

"I'm not having myself sent to bed. I'm as fit as a fiddle. I can still do everything. I'm going to get you some firewood from the shed."

"It's already in the laundry room. William brought it in. There's enough for a whole week."

"Nice lad. Except you have to pour beer into him from time to time. Taciturn, like most of the fishermen around here. At sea they don't teach you to talk, one of them said to me the other day in the tavern. You're too busy, he said. And if you have a bit of spare time once in a while there's always the sea around you that you mustn't ever take your eyes off. Shall I let Robert out?"

"Later," she says, "when we have company."

"You're being very mysterious. Who could it be except Ellen and Jack Robbins? Or William Cheever? Or are the children coming? About time too."

"They lead their own lives. But Kitty phoned the other day and said she'd soon be coming over for a while."

"You'd better hide the radio in that case. It may seem crazy, but you can't even trust your own children these days. Before you know it they let their tongues run away with them at school and you're in for it."

"The war has been over for a long time, Maarten. We're living in a free country, in America."

"You don't need to tell me where I live. I live in Gloucester, Massachusetts. The other day I was in the tavern and a fellow says to me, at sea they don't teach you to talk. What are you nodding your head for? You weren't there, were you?"

"Never mind."

"Ah, here's Robert. Shall we go for a walk, Robert?"

"In a while, Maarten, in a while. You'd better stay in now. We're going to have company in a minute."

"Company at this hour of the day? Or is it evening already?"

"Wait quietly, now."

"Who's coming, then?"

She does not reply.

As long as it isn't Karen. I wouldn't know what to say to her. She'd be sixty-five now, a ridiculous thought. Maybe she's dead. Imagine me sitting here thinking of someone who doesn't exist any longer. There's no way of knowing. I remember it so clearly, how I stood before her, naked and trembling like an aspen-leaf.

"Maarten."

"Bye, Aspen-leaf. I really must be off now. Otherwise I'll be much too late for my meeting."

"You don't have to go."

"Did they phone, then? Did Bahr phone?"

"Yes . . . he phoned."

"Why didn't you say so before?"

"You only mentioned it yourself just now. You don't have to go to work, Maarten. Lie down on the settee for a while."

"Yesyesyesyesyesyes." The weapon of politeness, secret and lethal. I lie down but in my mind I am standing up. By God, I will go on fighting against those waves, against those breakers inside my head. I slowly sway this way and that on the cushion someone slides under my head, and I start singing, it happens all by itself, softly and under my breath so Mama and Pop won't hear me in the living-room, I sing songs from which the words slowly slip away, I feel them slipping away from my head which turns heavily this way and that.

I hear women's voices coming from the kitchen. They are talking in English. Vera's voice and a voice I don't know, a soft, young, woman's voice. First I can distinguish only what the unfamiliar voice says, beautifully modulating the words. Patience and the correct medicines, the same environment as much as possible. Then I hear Vera.

"More than forty years I have been married to him. And then suddenly this. Usually these things happen more slowly, gradually. But with him it came all at once. I feel it has been sprung on me. It's cruel and unfair. Sometimes I get so angry and rebellious when I see him looking at me as if from another world. And then again I feel only sad and I would so much like to understand him. Or I just talk along with him and I feel ashamed afterwards. I'm glad you're here because it really gets on top of me at times, when I just can't bear watching it any more. At least now I'll be able to get out occasionally."

There is a moment of silence. I feel the tears running under my eyelids and down my cheeks.

"And sometimes, sometimes his face radiates perfect peace. As if he's happy. Like a child can be. Those moments are so brief I sometimes think I imagine them. But I know only too well what I see at such moments: someone who looks exactly like my husband of long ago. At your age it's difficult to understand that. But people like us live by their memories. If they don't have those any longer there's nothing left. I am afraid he is in the process of forgetting his whole life. And to live alone with those memories while he sits there . . . empty."

I press the palms of my hands against my ears, I don't want to hear it but I know it is true what is being said. I am being split open from inside. It is a process I cannot stop because I myself am that process. You think "I," "my body," "my mind," but these are only words. They used to protect me. Before I was like this. But now there is a greater force holding sway in me, which is not to be gainsaid. I don't want to think about it any more. I had better go and do some work. Work provides distraction. I must go through some reports for tomorrow. The text of reports reassures me, because of the inexorable peace and calm with which an un-reachable undersea reality is described in figures. As if that world were immobile, as if it could be measured.

The sun shines on the grain of the wooden leaf of the desk. No idea where I put those reports. Maybe they are still in my briefcase. I bend down, but my briefcase is not where it should be under the desk. Perhaps Vera put it somewhere else when she was clean-ing the room.

I stand up and go to the kitchen. In the doorway I pause. My legs tremble. A white woollen turtleneck sweater over which falls long blonde hair. I wave to Vera. I put my forefinger on my lips. Then she turns and fortunately I just manage to say, "Good morn-ing." How could it possibly have been Karen, fool that I am, where do such thoughts come from?

She gets up. She is surprisingly tall, with broad, practical hands. No rings. A bit heavy around the hips, where her jeans stretch in tight creases.

"Phil Taylor."

She speaks hurriedly, as if I were making her feel nervous. She wants to come and stay with us for a while, I gather. I nod amiably.

"Kitty and Fred aren't here," I say. "So you'll have the whole upper floor to yourself."

"Kitty and Fred?"

"My children."

Vera points at a carton of purchases standing on the draining-board. "Phil has already done the shopping. We're having roast beef tonight. Your favorite meat."

So she is called Phil. Lovely long blonde hair. A high, slightly rounded forehead. Now I suddenly remember why I came into the kitchen. "Have you seen my briefcase anywhere?"

"Not under the desk?"

"It's not there."

"I'll look for it for you."

"Look for what?"

"Your briefcase."

I turn abruptly and walk straight to the front room and sit by the table with my head in my hands. Something inside me thinks and then stops half-way. Starts on a totally different track and then halts again. Like a car engine that keeps stalling.

I get up and start walking. Using the choke, you might call it. Trying to get things going again. Robert raises himself slowly and lazily and shambles along beside me, rubbing against my legs. No wonder a dog wants to go out in this fine weather. I come to a halt with my knees pressing against the ribs of the radiator.

Spring hides in those bare branches. Birds will soon be returning from far away across the sea. Behind Vera's blue Datsun stands a bright green Chevrolet with a dented left pane . . . panel . . . sheet . . . metal . . . dent . . . bang . . . metal . . . fender.

"Goddammit!" I bang against the window with both fists.

"Mr. Klein!"

I turn, raise my eyebrows. Who is that? How did that girl get in here?

"Kitty isn't in. Or have you come for Fred? Are you a friend of my son?"

"Would you like us to take the dog for a walk together?"

"What about Vera?" (How panicky my voice sounds all of a sudden.)

"Her back is troubling her a bit."

Why am I always so timid? "I don't even know your name," I say. "And isn't it rather unusual, anyway, an old horse like me walking out with a pretty young filly like you? Are you a classmate of Kitty's?"

"My name is Phil Taylor," she says. "I've come to stay with you and your wife for a while."

"Oh, have you? I didn't know. But it's all right with me. I rather like having company actually."

"Shall we go, then?"

She goes to the hall and puts on a blue quilted parka. Then she helps me into my coat. She knows her manners. I watch her face from aside. A slightly plump nose, that's a pity. And her eyebrows are a little on the heavy side as well. Resolute chin. Usually such people have beautiful necks, but I cannot see that because of the high collar of her parka.

The girl goes to the front door. She unlocks it. "Where are we going?" I ask.

"To take Robert for a little walk. You say where."

Robert is standing beside me on the swept porch, wagging his tail. Behind us a young girl closes the door. I gingerly walk down the steps, stamp about with my black shoes on the snow-covered gravel path. I see the sharp footprints of a squirrel. At every hop, his tail has put an exclamation mark behind them. The girl put her arm through mine. She does it naturally, as if she were my daughter.

"It's slippery out," she says. "Where are we going?"

"To the stone man."

"The stone man?"

"Follow me."

She has put up the hood of her parka. Her blonde hair is hidden under the hood. You can smell the sea quite well from here. Seagulls stay at a sensible height when they see Robert running ahead of us. I wonder where we are going. There is something adventurous about it. On this side the coast is rocky and here and there steep. The paths to the beach are narrow but this blonde girl is holding me firmly.

"Vera is a wonderful person," she says all of a sudden, bluntly amid the bare pine trees.

"Oh, do you know her? Yes, she means everything to me. Every-thing. That's the only thing you sometimes worry about when you get older. That she might go before me. I don't think I could survive a winter like this on my own. Who would I have to talk to? We have done everything together, been through everything together. I was standing in the back yard one day, it was high summer, I remember there were birds singing all around me, and I saw her through the window, standing by the sink. She was cutting a loaf. I watched her. Slice after slice. A brown loaf, it was. That was all. That's the sort of thing I mean. Another person would see only a house, but everything is there: all the gestures, all the smells, all the words of my life. But now it's gone wrong. Every day something disappears, every day there's something gone. It leaks everywhere."

"Come, you forget a few things from time to time but in general you're perfectly healthy, aren't you?"

"Who's to say? Let's leave the subject alone, shall we?"

Robert dashes across the wet-gleaming rocks behind which the sea-water swirls and runs into gulleys between the carelessly heaped stones. Here and there, in a hollow, a stagnant puddle has formed which will presently evaporate when the sun comes out. The water along the shore looks dark from the algae and seaweed that grow against the underside of the rocks. I look across the flat slabs of stone; in places they are covered with greyish-white furry seaweed. I turn my back to the sea. This makes me feel better at once, more stable.

"Is the stone man somewhere near here? You seem to be looking for something."

"Did Vera tell you about him?"

"No, you did."

"Did I . . . ?"

"It doesn't matter."

"Here," I say, "you can see him from here. If you look to the right, to that rock jutting out into the sea. It's like a man lying on top of it, embedded in the stone, with his face turned towards the open sea. You see?"

A girl. Look at her. Peering. Screwing up her eyes a bit, like someone who is slightly short-sighted. She puts her hands into the pockets of her blue parka and you can tell from her face that she sees nothing but stone and water.

"Everybody sees something different," I say in order to console her. I can see him very clearly, but this may be because other people have pointed him out to me. The legend has it that he was ship-wrecked long ago. He gazes out to sea, trying to lure ships towards the shore where they will flounder on the rocks and he will have company at last. A typical sailor's yarn. All sailors are afraid of the shore, after all.

"I don't like the sea," says the girl. She looks across the bay, which is at its widest here. "I almost got drowned in it once."

"So did a colleague of mine," I say. "Only he didn't need the sea for it. A bathtub was enough for him. Maybe I could have saved him."

"Saved him? Were you there, then . . . when it happened?"

"No. I left, and then it happened."

"Someone saved me," she says. "Someone. I'd gone too far out. Back on the beach I lost consciousness. When I came to the man had disappeared. No one knew who he was. No one knew him."

"Poor Karl."

"Karl?"

"Do you know him? Karl Simic. That's how you pronounce it, Simmitch."

"Shall we go back?" she says.

"All we need to do is follow Robert," I say. "Do you have to be home before dark?"

"I'm coming with you."

"Are you staying for supper? Does Vera know?"

She nods. Vera might have told me. Too many things happen behind my back these days. It was the same at work towards the end. You were no longer taken altogether seriously. Just because you'd grown a day older. All respect and interest go by the board. I disengage my arm from hers.

"I want to walk on my own for a bit."

She remains close behind me. I quicken my pace in order to get back to Vera sooner. Only with her can I still have what can be called a "conversation." The others merely interrogate you or try to confuse you, lead you up the garden path.

Can't understand this. Vera lives here, doesn't she? And now she has suddenly vanished, nowhere to be found, while a young girl is frying meat in the kitchen. Someone ought to explain this to me. I have looked everywhere but she is nowhere. It's the right house, I'm sure. Anyway, Robert would be the first to notice that mistake. He is fast asleep in his old familiar spot, tired from the open air. So am I, actually, but I can't afford to take a nap now. Must stay awake. This question has to be answered first.

Dusk is already falling. Vera never stays at the library as late as this. And since when have we had a girl to help in the house? I've said it before, more and more things are being schemed behind my back. I don't like it a bit.

Three, five, six, one, the number of the library. I still know it by heart. No one answers. So they're already closed.

I walk into the kitchen and ask whoever she is whether she knows where Vera has gone.

"She's with Ellen Robbins," she says.

"That alters the situation."

I must admit it smells delicious in here. The girl goes with me to the living room. Asks if she may play the piano.

She plays from memory. And then, because of the music, everything suddenly becomes clear and lucid. Of course I knew all along who she was but I couldn't place her in this environment. That can happen, that you initially fail to recognize a person out of their usual context.

I pull a chair up and look at the strong ringless fingers as they seek their way effortlessly over the black and white keyes. How beautifully she plays! And then I do what I have always wanted to do but have never dared. She briefly goes on playing, but then she lifts my head from her lap and pushes me upright. In her fright she starts talking to me in English.

"You mustn't do that again. Otherwise I shall have to leave."

All in rapid English. The lesson is clearly at an end, although I haven't played a single note to her yet. She leads me to the settee and then goes to the kitchen.

I sit straight up on the settee. For a moment it is as silent in the house as in a diving bell. Or does this silence well up inside me? I get up, go to the television set standing on a low oak table, and switch it on.

I watch a game with a lot of laughing people in a hall and constantly changing numbers at the bottom of the screen. Although I don't understand the game very well, I am clearly so engrossed in it that I haven't heard Vera come in. Maybe she walked on tiptoe because she thought I had fallen asleep in front of the television. She sits down beside me on the settee and asks if I had a good walk with Phil. So she knows about this.

"How do you know her?"

"Through Dr. Eardly. She's come to stay with us for a while."

"I thought she was a friend of Kitty's. She's so young still."

"She'll stay with us for a while. So I can take it a bit easier."

"Have you been to the library?"

"No, I was with Ellen Robbins."

"Your hair looks different. Have you been to the hair-dresser?"

"No, no. I've had it like this for ages."

I do not reply. This kind of floundering conversation is on the increase. I keep missing the links. When you pay close attention and listen carefully, a fair amount can be reconstructed, enough to keep up the appearance to the outside world that you understand everything, but sometimes there are such large gaps that you can fill them only be remaining silent, by pretending you haven't heard.

Vera gets up and goes to the kitchen. So she's called Phil, that blonde girl, Phil. It is three degrees on Pop's outdoor Heidensieck thermometer. Sparrows are scratching among crisp, curly brown leaves underneath the bare shrubs along the drive. In the bend of Field Road the mustard-colored school bus from Gloucester comes along. Behind the misty windows children are hitting one another with schoolbags. They shriek and shout, they thump on the glass with their hands, chase one another down the aisle. I can see them but not hear them.

The bus drops them at the stop, and then returns empty by way of Eastern Point to Atlantic Road, to the municipal parking lot by the harbor. I watch the children clambering out of the bus—Tom's little Richard is last—and running away in all directions like colorful blobs among the tree trunks. Richard. In his dark blue striped woolly hat he looks down the road. Then he lets the bag slide from his back, holds it in his right hand and walks, limping slightly, into the wood. At each step the outspread peacock tail on his back moves. With his free hand he knocks snow from the branches, the last snow of the winter. If he were to turn his head this way he would be able to see me. Then he disappears from my field of vision.

Here in Gloucester the school is modern, with large windows through which the children can look out over the bay with its fishing boats or at the mist banks rolling across the sea, swallowing up everything except the flickering lamp of the lighthouse on the low, rocky islet in the middle of the bay, Ten Pound Island. My own grade school looked more like a brick fortress with tall narrow windows. Class by class you were marched in from the school yard through the solid oak door, up the stairs that smelled of soft soap, and into the classroom with its odor of chalk and old floorcloths, and in winter of wet clothes and briquettes. When I look back on my gradeschool days it is as if I were invisible for six years somewhere at the back of the class. Invisible as I listened to the screeching of the chalk on the grey chalkboard. Pop sometimes went to the school to ask how I was getting on because I never said anything. I remember he came home in a rage one day because the teacher could form no picture of anyone of my name. It was not until I started studying law that I became a little less invisible, started to talk and very occasionally, at beery debating club evenings, to argue. That was how I came to be invited to join Jan Tholen and Paul Verdassdonk at a party by one of the canals. There, I met Vera.

I was slightly tipsy, only very slightly, but just enough to give a lengthy account of a play I had seen. *The Seagull* I think it was. She was sitting on a pouf with her knees together, her hands clasped over her narrow kneecaps. She was wearing a tight grey skirt and a black sweater. From somewhere in a corner of the room, lamplight fell on the side of her jaw. Strange that of those first moments I remember mostly her kneecaps and her chin, the bony parts. She only listened. She listened while looking at me without interruption. For the first time in my life I was not shy. I returned her gaze. I don't know whether the others in the room noticed. The room, the others, I have completely forgotten them. Left in my memory are Vera and I, looking at each other, until long after I had finished talking. There was something quite shameless and exciting about it. We penetrated each other's eyes. Love at first sight. That is the phrase. But actually we wanted to know, in one look, each other's past life, down to the smallest detail. The fact that before this meeting she had not known me, had been ignorant of my existence, seemed at once unbearable to me. She was no longer allowed to have anyone else. Her father, her mother, any brothers or sisters she might have, her bosom friends, I effaced them from her life with my gaze and gave her a new name. Later I took her on my bike to the house of an aunt in the eastern part of the city where she was staying. For half an hour we stood pressed against each other in a cold stone doorway. The following afternoon I received a telegram from Alkmaar. "Come at once." Like the urgent call of someone dying. That night I slept with her in the room of a friend of hers. We mated, that is the only word, fiercely, as if our lives depended on it. Now life has begun, I thought, now a life has begun of which you had no inkling. Three months later we were married. I had to convince my parents it was not a shotgun wedding.

"Maarten. Don't you feel anything?"

She points at the scorch patches on my knees. Now that she has mentioned it I can smell it, but I still don't feel anything. The fact that you can stand for so long with your legs against a radiator without feeling the heat cannot, of course, be explained by my reply that I was wrapped in thought. Can you be so deeply wrapped in thought that it makes you numb? It is an annoying incident, especially because I can't think for the life of me what I was thinking about. I promise her I will change my pants at once.

I undress and crawl between the cold sheets. I lie absolutely still with my knees drawn up until I am completely warm. Only then do I turn over on my side. Just when I am lying comfortably Vera

comes to wake me. Is it morning? Why all this hurry? And since
when don't I put my clothes on by myself? She kneels in front of
me and ties my shoelaces.

"Get up."

"You're just like my mother when we used to go into town once
a year to buy clothes."

"I'm not your mother."

As if I didn't know. What's the matter with her this morning?

Roast beef for breakfast? And who is this girl at the table? From
her conduct I gather she knows who I am. Better wait and see.
Maybe Vera will mention her name or she might make some
remark that gives me a clue as to her identity. The Simic method
makes no provision for this. It serves only to make you invisible.
I have to yawn heartily a couple of times. I apologize but they
pretend they haven't noticed. (That is very kind of those two
women.)

I am not very hungry, but then, who would ever think of serving
roast beef for breakfast? There, they are talking now, a conversation
has started up between those two!

"Would you like some salad with it, Phil?"

Good, so that young one is called Phil. Join in straight away
now.

"Don't you feel rather hot in that woollen sweater, Phil?" I say
to the blonde girl.

She shakes her head, she has her pretty mouth full just now.
Pity, I wouldn't have minded seeing her breasts. Vera used to have
such beautiful ones, too, when she was young. And even now I
still love to put my face between them.

They carry on eating and say nothing more. Every now and
again they look at me as if expecting something of me. Vera gives
the blonde girl another slice of roast beef. Well prepared, blood-

red in the middle, that's how it should be. You can leave that to Vera.

"I've made a room ready for you upstairs," she says to the girl, so I gather she is staying the night. Maybe she is a friend of Kitty's who has called in unexpectedly, thinking Kitty would be in. She is attractive. Full lips, the upper lip with a classical curve, and a high, slightly bulbous forehead. She reminds me of someone. Blue eyes, bright blue. Usually blue eyes are pale, mixed with a little grey, like mine, but not these ones. They look and they see. I would dare to speak to her, but as I don't know her name I say nothing.

She knows me, though. I can tell from her whole behavior. Stalemate. I wait for a breakthrough. That is what is so annoying. More and more often I have to wait, be on the alert. What used to be self-evident (at least I have to assume it was) has now become enigmatic. And I don't want to keep asking questions all the time. So I wait, meanwhile slowly and painstakingly chewing a piece of meat.

Suddenly they have finished eating and immediately afterwards (the ladies seem to be quickening their tempo) there is coffee. I am given something with my coffee, a green capsule, or is it candy?

"Swallow it in one go, Maarten, don't bite on it."

If Vera says so it must be all right.

"I thought it was candy," I say by way of excuse.

The girl examines her nails. She seems to be bored. Whatever is she doing here, having coffee with two old people?

"You can turn the television on if you like," I say to her.

She does so at once, and this makes me feel content. I have been able to please her in a small way. She sits down on the settee, arms spread out wide along the back, her legs crossed. She is wearing green knitted slippers on her feet. That surprises me, at this time of year.

"How are you feeling now, Maarten?"

"I couldn't tell you. Honestly, I'm sorry. I really don't know."

"Try to say what you are thinking."

"Everything happens in jolts and jerks. There is no flowing movement any longer, as there used to be. Nowhere. The day is full of cracks and holes. So to speak. No, really, honestly. It's no good any longer." (Who or what forms these creaking sentences, which I try to utter—by means of interjections and insertions— more or less casually?)

"Who's that strange girl there?"

"But Phil isn't a stranger. You went for a walk with her this afternoon."

"Oh yes, of course. So it is evening now. That's a stroke of luck isn't it!" (Perhaps I pat her on the shoulder a bit too hard, sometimes I am not in full control of that either, dividing my strength among various activities; taking hold of a glass much too gently so it smashes to pieces, grabbing a towel as though it weighed ten pounds.)

"Tomorrow is another day!" (This kind of sentence presents the least difficulty; proverbs, set phrases pop out all by themselves, with them my speech comes closest to normal talking.)

I get up and wave to a blonde girl who cheerfully waves back from the settee without moving her wrist.

Suddenly my body reels with sleep. I don't even bother to brush my teeth.

I wake up with a feeling as though I had drunk large quantities of beer. I go to the toilet but only a hesitant, thin hot trickle comes out. I shuffle back on bare feet through the dark passage. At the top of the stairs I see light burning under Kitty's door. Softly I climb the stairs, seeking support from the banisters.

Father and daughter, that is a very different bond from the one you have with a son. With Fred my contact is more choppy, but I like talking to Kitty.

When I enter her room she slaps her hands on her bare breasts in alarm. I smile and sit down on the edge of her bed. "It's only your father," I say.

She slides out of the bed on the other side, in her slip, snatches a blue T-shirt from the chair on which she has hung her clothes and quickly puts it on. (And suddenly, in a flash; this is the last time you see this—how Kitty with her breasts jutting out and a hollow back pulls down a T-shirt tightly to below her darkly caving navel.)

"Yes," I say resignedly, "there comes a time when daughters don't want to be bare any more in front of their own fathers."

From the corner of the room, beside the chair, she looks at me thoughtfully, holding her head at a slant. A strand of her blond hair falls past her left shoulder across the T-shirt. On the pillow lies an open book which she has been reading. *The Heart of the Matter* by Graham Greene.

She walks around the bed and pulls me up with gentle force. "Come," she says in English. "It's the middle of the night. You must go to sleep."

"Oh, is it as late as that?"

Arm in arm we walk down the stairs. There is something stately, something solemn about it, as if I am going to give this girl, whom I do not know, in marriage to an as yet unknown bridegroom. Vera wakes up when the girl switches on the light in the bedroom. She talks to Vera as if I were a stranger.

"He was wandering around," she says, again in English. The way your parents used to speak when they didn't want you to know about something.

Together they tuck me in bed. I am not sick, but I let them do as they please. Behind my closed eyelids I see the light go out again. I am lying on my back. Beside me Vera turns over on to her side. At first I don't hear her breathing, but then she suddenly sighs profoundly a couple of times and I hear the deep, regular breathing of a sleeping person.

Nearly fifty years we have been lying side by side like this. It is almost impossible to comprehend what that means. The feeling of being two communicating vessels. Her moods, her thoughts; can almost read them in her face, like Pop read the temperature on his thermometer. A graph of my love for Vera? An idea that Pop would not have understood. Once he spoke of his love for Mama, whom he always called "wife." That was when they had been married for forty years and he gave an after-dinner speech, a glass of red wine in his hand. He compared Mama to a piece of music, to the adagio from Mozart's fourteenth piano sonata. "Just as clear, bright and unfathomable." That was what he said. And after that I played the adagio on our out-of-tune black piano and the tears came to Mama's eyes, Pop told me, for I couldn't see it myself. I can't sleep because I need to pee. Then it's no use remaining in bed, I know that from experience.

Someone has left the light on in the hall. Clear, bright and unfathomable. Without women the world would be drab and violent, says Pop. "Maarten, will you play what I mean but for which my words are inadequate?"

This sentence is the signal for me to walk to the piano. We have agreed on this in advance, Pop and I.

I sit down at the piano, raise my hands above the keys and search. I can't find the beginning. Always I see it before me but not now. Perhaps I ought to make light first. I switch on the wall lamp and stand looking at the keys for a while. Then I sit down again. I close my eyes, hoping that the distances between the keys will return, that I will feel the first notes in my fingers again, but nothing happens. I get up and look for the sonata among the pile of sheet music on the piano. I put the album on the stand and leaf through it until I have found the adagio. There they are, the notes. But they won't come off the page and into my fingers. It would be terrible to disappoint them all. Perhaps I ought to limber up first, just a few notes, so the beginning will suddenly slip back into my fingers. As long as I have the beginning, the rest will come all by itself. Harder and harder I press the black and white keys, more and more keys I press in order to find that one damned beginning. But there are thousands of possibilities. Yet I must find the beginning, I must!

"Maarten, what's the matter? Why are you crying?"

Vera in her dark blue dressing-gown, her brown hair in a wild mop around her head.

"The beginning, I can't find the beginning."

I hear footsteps overhead, look up at the ceiling.

"That's Phil," she says, looking up with me. "You've woken her up with your playing."

I don't know who she is talking about, but of course I am sorry. "I was practicing for the wedding and I can't find the beginning any more."

Someone enters the room. A young girl in jeans and a blue T-shirt. She is barefoot, which is odd for this time of year.

"Maarten always plays the adagio from Mozart's fourteenth piano sonata from memory. He's known it by heart for years. And now he suddenly can't find the beginning any more."

The girl nods sleepily. I can see it doesn't interest her in the least (and rightly, for what a ridiculous situation this is, an old man playing the piano in the middle of the night in his pyjamas).

"I'll get something for him," she says and leaves the room. Vera goes to the record player beside the television. She crouches by the record shelf. I feel cold, and I want some beer. I go to the kitchen.

Standing in the middle of the kitchen, with the handle of the refrigerator door in my hand, I suddenly hear the adagio coming from the living room. Clear, bright and unfathomable. Slowly, almost solemnly, I enter the room to the rhythm of the music.

In the centre of the room stands Vera, amid the furniture. I have never seen her like this, so forlorn and so small as she stands there barefoot on the wooden floor in her dark shiny dressing-gown among the gleaming furniture. Her hands seem to be groping for a hold in the air.

I know I must have done something wrong. I want to go up to her and ask her, in order to bridge the distance between her and me. But then I am seized from behind and feel, right through my pyjama sleeve, a dull stab of pain shooting up in my left upper arm.

Vera is sitting on the settee. She is listening to Mozart's adagio. She has tears in her eyes. Like this she looks exactly like Mama.

I am led away by a stranger but I suppose it must be all right if Vera is suddenly so happy again. Therefore I smile and nod to the young woman beside me. I behave as though this were the way life is supposed to be.

A huge bed. Lying utterly hopelessly the wrong way round in it. Terrible stink here. My ass smarts, icy cold buttocks I have. I try to raise myself but my ankles are tied down. What has happened to me? Where have I been moved to? Where is this bed? Now?

I recognize all those things around me, sure I do. Behind a closed door sounds an unfamiliar female American voice: "Fill the bath up."

Jesus, have I befouled the matrimonial bed? How do you like that! It's not my fault. If you tie a man to his bed! Strapped to the bars, I ask you. Who has done that to me? And where is Vera? I call out but you can bet nobody will come. I can't reach the straps that are cutting into my ankles. I wish I could bear the smell of my own shit as well as Robert.

"Robert! Robert!"

No one. Perhaps they've all gone. Leaving me to rot here in this bed. I hear water running. In a minute the place will be flooded and I can't get out of my bed. I kick about. The bed creaks but the straps don't give an inch.

Somewhere a door opens. I don't dare look because I have no idea who's coming. And because I am ashamed to be lying here like a beast in my own muck. I keep my eyes tightly shut. I hear someone retching. Feel how hands strip the pyjamas from my body. They want me to move forward. Must open my eyes now and see an old man in the mirror, an old man with a slack wrinkly belly streaked with shit. I smile with relief. At least that isn't me!

Two women lift me into a bath tub, an old one and a young one.

I lie in this water as if I no longer had a body. Only where they touch me, wash me, does it briefly exist again.

Careful, I say to the younger one who dares not look at me because she is embarrassed by a male organ that floats in the soapy water and now rises, purple and gently quivering.

"Don't mind about it," I say. "The regime under the belt, Chauvas used to call it. Why do we cover it up so anxiously, why is there such a taboo on it? Do you know what Chauvas thought? Chauvas said the following: May I have your attention, please, because this cannot be put in the minutes, as you will understand, certainly not by lady secretaries. We are afraid of sexuality because it undermines the basis of our whole society: the idea that every person is a unique individual with an organized life. But if every man can, in principle, go to bed with every woman and vice versa then all those stories about predestination, preordination, destiny and eternal love are so much poppycock. We are floating through space like particles, plus ones and minus ones. And where these meet, a fusion may occur. Everybody knows this, but suppresses it. Man is not capable of philanthropic sex because in that case there would be no point in doing anything except this."

I grab hold of the stiff prick in the water and feel it is my own. From fright and shame I let go.

They pull me upright. They make no reply to my words as the younger one dries me and the other one tries to pull a pair of underpants over my rough damp buttocks, in order to withdraw the subject of the conversation—which fortunately becomes limp again—as quickly as possible from sight. Then they bundle me into a dressing-gown.

"I don't have to go to bed, do I? Did you understand me, madam?" I say to the older one, who looks rather dishevelled with her damply drooping brown curls and her wrinkled neck.

"We've read Freud, too," says the younger one sharply.

The arrogance of youth. Think they know something about life when they've read a few books.

"Look around you," I say. "Not that I approve of Chauvas's conduct. On the contrary. But no one can accept that what he calls his life has been the only possible life for him. It could have been different. If you had chanced to put your prick in a totally different cunt, for instance. Or even stronger; if your father had screwed someone other than your mother or your mother a different man, you wouldn't even have been here in the same form."

"Go and rinse out your mouth." It is Vera who says this.

"All right," I say. "I will. Right away."

They let go of me so I can reach the washstand. I pick up the toothbrush and look in the mirror. There isn't anyone there. Everything is white. I throw the toothbrush away. They take hold of me. I let myself be led away, away from the white of that mirror.

□

Want to eat more. They won't let me. Simply take my plate away. How do you like that? They are strangers here so they give no answer when I ask a question. The simplest things: time, season, what are the plans for the day.

The fingers of my left hand are numb. Put the hand on the table, palm upward. Move my fingers. Clench, relax; clench, relax. Compared with the right hand: as if there's no current going through it any longer. Rub ... rub ... rub.

Thumping footsteps, suddenly very close by. Hurts my ears. Parts of the body are oversensitive, others totally insensitive.

Jump out of my skin with fright when suddenly someone is standing by the sink. A small woman in a lemon-colored apron. She lets water run from a tap on to white plates. I ask her where Vera is but I get no answer. Her neck is wrinkled and brown from the open air. I don't know where I am.

Grab hold of the edge of the table and let go. And again. There is activity in the space around me that is totally detached from me. Sound of water gurgling away through a wastepipe. Very successful. Pity it stops—maybe we can imitate it.

Want to be near water, very near to water, hold this numb left hand in a fast running shallow brook. Sit motionless on the bank and then, suddenly see, caught in a quivering patch of sun on the silver-white sandy riverbed, the slim shadow of a fish (where does this image come from, from what depths, it is as clear as if I could touch it; it is sad but true: you, Maarten, were once that little boy sitting by the side of that stream!).

A young woman with long straight blonde hair is sitting opposite me at the table. I nod to her, although I do not understand her presence. She asks me why I am rubbing the table with my hand.

I look and feel only now that the hand is rubbing across the red dotted oil-cloth (how long has this been going on?).

When I have raised my head again I must quickly force a smile. "I have become an old man. Quite suddenly, it seems," I say. She shakes her head, but I know better.

She gets up and the red of her sweater becomes even redder than the dots on the oil-cloth. She pulls me to my feet. How annoying to have to let go of the table. I grab her hand and she leads me away through an open door into a different space. There stands Pop's desk! I remember being allowed to draw at it on Sundays. A white paper on a baize-green blotter covered in the inkstains and scribbles of Pop's blotted letters. When you looked for a long time you saw all kinds of things in them: animals, faces. I used to copy them.

"As a boy I liked to crawl under that desk with a book. *The Travels and Adventures of Captain Hatteras. Captain Hatteras in Search of the North Pole.* They all dreamed of that in the days of Jules Verne. I used to like reading about it as a boy. Amundsen, Nansen, Captain Hatteras. Did you know he went mad in the end, and was locked up in an institution? I have never forgotten the ending of *The Ice Desert.* He is walking in the garden of the institution, which is surrounded by a high brick wall, always in the same direction, northward. Until he bumps into the wall. There, his arms stretched out against the bricks, he remains motionless for hours. And then I put my hands on the wood of Pop's desk and close my eyes and try to imagine what it is like to be Captain Hatteras, alone in a desert of ice floes."

"Your father is dead."

"Yes, well, stands to reason, doesn't it, if you're as old as I am."

Again the edge of a table. And a chair. (Was it already there or has it just been pushed forward?) I sit down. Notice that the rubbing has resumed. Not unpleasant, actually.

"My favorite place to sit was under the desk. I'd push the chair back and crawl underneath the desk with a book. *The Travels and*

Adventures of Captain Hatteras. In the end he went mad from all that whiteness around him. He ended up in an institution. While he was there he used to walk all the time in a northerly direction. Until he couldn't go any further. Until he ran into a wall. Then he would stand still for hours."

Outside, a woman walks down a snowy garden to a blue car. She waves. I wave back. People are friendly here, that cannot be denied. She starts the car and reverses out of a drive (the view would be less empty, easier to cope with, if trees, like people, all had a name of their own).

A girl opposite me asks why I am rubbing the wood with my left hand.

"Otherwise I can't see the hand any longer."

"See?"

"Yes."

"Otherwise you can't feel your left hand any longer?"

"More or less. Yes, exactly. As I said."

She has picked up an oblong book and opens it. Black pages. She turns the book over and pushes it towards me.

"No pictures, please."

"But it's your own photo album."

In order to please her I leaf through it. Wedding photos. Photos of children. I turn the album round and point at one of them.

"I never see them any more. Kitty was supposed to come over. Have you met her?"

"I'm sure she'll come."

"And Fred even less. You never see them any more. They're no longer your children." (Try not to cry now.)

"What's this?" She puts her finger on a photograph of a man walking beside a wide river. Across the water there is a row of big houses, strung along the bank which lies in the shade. The man is walking in the sun along a quay wall. He looks sideways into the camera.

"A river," I say. "The Rhine, maybe?"

"But who is that man?"

"Could it be me?"

"Of course. You haven't changed that much."

"Yes, now that you say so, it is me. But I'm not so sure about the river. The Rhine?"

"And who is that?"

A woman in a little black hat with fluttering veil, pushing a baby carriage. Old-fashioned, tailored two-piece suit.

"Mama I suppose. My mother, I mean, I beg your pardon. With me." I look from the photograph to her face. "Or am I wrong?"

"Have another look."

"I honestly don't know just now."

"It's your wife. It's Vera."

"Please put the book away."

"You must go on looking. If you go on looking and you think of her very hard, you're sure to recognize her again."

"She has changed. Or maybe I am the one who has changed. She was a beautiful woman."

"She is still beautiful now."

I nod. Yes, she will remain beautiful for ever, with those green eyes behind that veil pleased forever by the wind.

"The waters broke," I say. "All of a sudden. As if it was raining. She clutched at my shoulders. I got drenched."

Again I look at the photograph of the woman with the baby carriage, at the veil that seems to want to fly away, at her narrow, hopeful face. Slowly and cautiously I nod. Then I start to talk. A story. A story about the woman with the hat and the veil. Vera. I place her with the baby carriage on the edge of Amsterdam.

That is where she lives. I talk about the child in the carriage, who cannot be seen in the photograph but who is my son Fred in the story. I talk about the fields, the glasshouses, the ditches and the footbridges, which lie outside the rectangle of the photograph. I talk about the time in which the photograph was taken, the last year of the war. This does not altogether tally with the tailored suit, but this girl sitting here won't know that, she belongs to a generation born long after the war and in another continent. She nods and she listens. I talk. About the blocked sewers (because the Germans had turned off the electricity in the pumping stations) so that everywhere in the streets deep shit holes were being dug that stank horribly and created a real risk of infectious diseases like cholera and typhoid. I talk about old, stooping Mr. Mastenbroek on the third floor who died of starvation two days before the liberation. You can't imagine that now, I say. What hunger is like. That dull, gnawing feeling, which resided not only in your stomach but everywhere. All your thoughts were governed by it. I talk of the arrival of the Canadians and Americans. Eisenhower's and Churchill's triumphal tour of the city in an open limousine. How I stood among the crowds with Fred on my shoulders and tears running down my cheeks. About the freedom celebrations, the first bar of chocolate, the biscuit porridge (thick and nourishing and at first too rich for my stomach, which for months had feasted only on sugarbeet and fried slices of tulip bulb). How everyone fell in love with life again, with one another, how many children were born in the Netherlands roughly a year after that 5 May. (I talk and talk and it is as if I am talking myself out of history, as if this were a book from which I am reading, or a text I know by heart; one thing is clear: what you tell you lose. Forever. Abruptly I fall silent and look around in alarm.)

□

Robert is not lying in his usual place. I ask a girl walking about where Robert, my dog is.

"Vera has taken him with her to Gloucester."

"But he has to be taken out for a walk at this time."

"Your wife will see to that."

"How long will she be away?"

"Not long."

"Do you know where Robert is?"

"Gone to Gloucester with your wife. In the car."

"Why didn't she say she was going? Is that why you're here?"

"In a way."

"I don't mind if you go home. I don't need to be looked after, you know. On the contrary, I rather like being on my own."

"I'll stay for a while, anyway."

"As you like. But tell me who you are first."

"Phil Taylor."

"The name doesn't ring a bell, but I've always had a bad memory for names. Phil. I suppose you must be a friend of my daughter's, are you? My daughter doesn't live here, though. Never has. You never see them any more."

"She'll come."

"Do you think so? Pop always reproached me that I visited him so seldom. And then he dies and no amends can ever be made. That is the worst of it, believe you me, when someone dies. Those that are left behind have forever fallen short. All guilt feelings are based on that."

"Would you like us to go for a little walk?"

"No. I'm waiting for the spring. It can't be long now. I don't mind telling you that I hate the winters here. In November when you hear the foghorn of the lighthouse near here wailing all day, you know it has started again. The cold, the dark, the snow, carrying logs. Have you seen the dog anywhere? His name is Robert."

"He's gone with your wife."

"I like that! That's against the agreement. I'm the one who takes the dog out here."

"He wanted to go with her."

"I used to be able to take him out only at weekends, but now I have plenty of time. He's getting rather old. The hair around his snout is getting quite grey."

"Do you mind if I watch television for a while?"

"Of course not, dear. Make yourself at home."

Yes. I ought to go and visit Pop some time. Of course he'll start talking about the war, as usual. The same old stories about hunger, journeys, rheumatism and his neighbor who joined the Nazi Defense and whom he never looked in the face again. And when he has finished talking about the war he winds his old portable phonograph and puts on Beethoven's second piano concerto. A complete album of big heavy shellac records. I ought to give him my record player. He'd love that. There's an empty carton in the kitchen. I think it would fit in it exactly.

A young woman (where has she suddenly sprung from, is the front door open by any chance?) tries to push me away from the record player.

"I will not be prevented, miss. My father sits at home with one of those old wind-up phonographs, and music is the only comfort and refuge left to him. Clear, bright and unfathomable. Perhaps you could lend me a hand packing it."

"Your father is dead."

It is with good reason that her face wears a somewhat shameful, perplexed expression.

"That is most unkind of you, what you said then."

I turn and walk to the window. Behind me sounds soft violin music. I don't know the piece but it is pleasant to listen to. I feel the damp window pane with my hands. Here comes Robert, belting along among the trees. I turn around with a jerk. "Open up double quick! Robert has found us!"

The blonde girl from earlier (so I can remember her for a while at any rate) gets up and goes to the hall. I go back to the record player and look at the black plastic arm, which moves slowly through the grooves of a rotating disc towards the hole in the centre of the sea-blue label. I see only the rotation and every now and then a groove rising briefly. I crouch so as to be closer to the movement. As if of its own accord, my head begins to spin too.

"Poppa, I'll come and see you soon. As soon as Vera is back we'll come."

Robert comes and stands beside me. I put my arm around his neck. So I squat together with the dog close to the record player until my knees give with fatigue and someone behind me is so kind as to help me to my feet. Robert's dark brown tail wags as we walk to the front door together. Vera is standing in the hall with her coat on.

"Wait," I say, "I'll get my coat, too. We really should go and see Pop. We haven't been there for ages."

She shakes her head, looks timidly at the rope-colored mat on which she is standing as though on an island.

"We can't, Maarten. Your father is dead."

I nod. I understand. Tears run down my cheeks.

"You're all so good to me." I sob. They tell me I should lie down for an hour or so. I am given a cup of warm milk and a capsule, against my grief for Pop, they say, which still goes on stirring inside me without forming thoughts or tears. It is more like a cool brightness, as in an unfurnished room.

Lying in bed I look out, into the bare woods. Among the thin, straight trunks of the pines and birches and the dead branches on the ground, the snow creeps slowly into the soil. The wood sucks up the snow and uses if for its new leaves and buds that are still hidden in the snow-covered branches. Any moment now, spring can break out. That happens very suddenly here. You wake up one morning. An age-old scent of humus and leaves rises from the ground and penetrates into the house through the cracks. You open the window wide. What you hear is not the cheeky solitary sound of a single stray squawking crow, but an incessant chorus of chirping and twittering. Small songbirds that have returned to the wood in their thousands.

I must go outside, I must be there when it happens, walk among the trees, on the springy ground. Hear the dead branches breaking underfoot with a crackle. Walk among the dark mossy boulders and rocks, that glaciers left on this spit of land millions of years ago. "But there is one problem." I whisper so as not to be heard. They won't let me go from here. Maybe they mean well, the ladies who live here, but I must do what my heart tells me. Fortunately, they have their television on loud, so it should be easy. The door to the living room is closed, a stroke of luck. A dance orchestra shrieks up into the air with all its trumpets at once as I softly open the door and close it again and turn right, straight into the wood.

I follow a narrow path which you can find only when you know where it runs. It really exists only because I know it. In this way I avoid the houses of people who might be able to see me.

Quite chilly still. A coat would have been welcome. Yet I do not go back. The boulders sticking up from the ground stubbornly show their white-veined surfaces. They inspire me with awe. They control this spit of land, hold it in check. Above me the sky is such a hard blue that I don't dare look at it. The path curves to the left and then gradually descends to the coast.

The dead wood is still too wet to break under my feet, it merely bends. I sniff and smell the sea. The white scent. There can hardly be breakers today, at least I don't hear the splashing of waves, although I must be quite near now.

I stumble and graze my right hand on a rough pine trunk. Here and there the snow has been blown up into a thick bank so that you can no longer see the projecting roots of trees. I lick the graze and see the rope-colored slopes of the dunes through the last trees. In places they are still covered with snow.

Low, hard shrubs and dry thistles prick me through the cloth of my pants. Better stay at the foot of the dunes, try to cross them from one dip to the next, in wide curves.

My God, how cold. I would like to sit down but the ground is so hard. If only I could see our cottage at last. Pop explained to me once how you can determine your direction with reference to the position of the sun, but I have forgotten how to do it. Brambles stick out of the snow in a stiff tangle of branches. Here and there I see the footprints of birds, and little heaps of dark, dried-up rabbit droppings. The low light stings my eyes. I must be near the sea now. Then I can follow the shoreline and cut across the beach to our cottage where Mama is sure to be getting worried. Maybe Pop has already gone out to look for me. I want to be found. I want to go home.

Suddenly something crunches under my feet. The road, the shell path! Now I'll soon be there. I am so happy I have found the way that I break into a trot. Then I see part of the mouse-grey roof appear behind a dune.

I almost trip on the steps to the porch. I grab at the step nearest the front door which gives, opens all by itself, as if someone had seen me coming and opened the door for me. I walk into the room. A white lacquered table, four chairs. They're not at home. There is only my briefcase leaning against a table leg. I bend down, open the briefcase. A hammer, a screwdriver. I place them in front of me on the table and stare first at the tools, then out of the window. It seems as if the hammer and screwdriver are saying in all their simplicity: you are alone, Maarten, alone. I look round me. On one of the wooden walls hangs a family portrait behind glass. A man in the uniform of an American soldier, his cap merrily pushed back on his short-cropped hair. A young woman with a wide, painted mouth carrying a baby on her arm. Our Lady of Good Voyage. A girl with pigtails is holding her right hand, the heel of one of her little patent leather shoes resting on the toe of the other. They look at me in a cheerful, admonishing way, but I do not recognize them. How did I come here? Incomprehensible. Like this briefcase here. I take the hammer and the screwdriver and put them into the briefcase. Then I hear the sound of a car engine. I stand up, take the briefcase and go outside.

Standing on the porch I clutch the briefcase with both hands against my stomach. The sound approaches fast over the hills; low and throbbing and then suddenly with a high-pitched shriek when the invisible driver changes gear. Then I see the broad ribbed nose of an army-green jeep popping up above one of the dunes. For a moment the jeep stands on the top, droning. Then it slowly rolls down towards me, leaving broad wheel tracks in the sand. The driver wears a black woolly sweater and jeans. On his head he has a moss-green cap. Boots and black gloves. Beside him sits a pale little boy in a bright yellow jacket. The man drives the jeep in a skillful curve alongside the balustrade of the porch.

"Mr. Klein," he calls out twice in succession, as if I didn't know who I was. Cautiously I shuffle down the steps and walk towards the jeep. The man gets out, pulls a plaid rug from the back, puts it around my shoulders and helps me into the jeep. When I am seated my jaws begin to chatter.

"I was working in the lighthouse when I saw you, Mr. Klein. Had you lost your way? You were tramping about the dunes in such strange twists and turns. I thought, what's that fellow doing there?"

"Wandered away from home, clearly." It sounds as if I am talking about someone else. Then I see the briefcase in my lap. "I'd forgotten my briefcase. I'd gone to collect my briefcase."

"Mr. Klein," says the young man with the blond springy hair that sticks out from under his cap in all directions, "I'll take you home. Straight away. Before you catch cold, without a coat on. What were you doing all by yourself?"

"A little stroll. I didn't have the dog with me. Forgotten. That's why."

These words do not really belong to me. Every now and then the little boy looks over his shoulder at me with big frightened eyes. He does not answer when I ask him his name, but perhaps he cannot hear me because of the noise of the engine. There is a blue peacock embroidered on the back of his jacket. A blue peacock with a fan-shaped tail full of dark eyes that stare at me steadily. I turn my head away, preferring to look into the wood with its blown-down trees and broken branches. In the bends I have to let go of my briefcase and grab hold of the metal back of the driver's seat in front of me.

When the jeep stops in front of my house Vera comes out on to the veranda. How thin she is! The American helps me get out. I hold the rug tightly around me for I still feel dreadfully cold.

"Maarten!" She takes my hand and drops it again at once. She shouldn't do that. I want to take hers again but she walks over to the American who has stayed beside his jeep. She shakes hands with him and also with the little boy. She talks to the man who waves his black-gloved hands dismissively in front of his chest and jumps back into the jeep. As he reverses he waves with one hand and I wave back from the veranda, until the jeep has disappeared from sight among the trees, past a bend in Field Road.

"At last," I say to Vera as she comes up the steps. "At last the time has come, darling." I follow her into the house and put my briefcase under the coat stand.

"It really can't go on like this any longer, Maarten!"

I enter a room and take stock of the interior. Strange, how people put chairs and tables and cupboards at random around a room. As a result I cannot decide where to sit down. Maybe it is also because of the cold. My fingers tingle as if I had just come back from ice skating.

Vera wants to take the rug away from me but I hold it tightly by two corners around my neck.

"The American gave it to me."

She lets go. "Maarten," she says, "what have you been up to? Where are your thoughts, for God's sake?"

Where are my thoughts? A coming and a going. No one knows where from and where to. But one thing is certain: what we have been waiting for all these months has happened at last.

"Thank God they have come at last. Five years we've had to wait for them. It's still cold outside but it will slowly get warmer. I was allowed to sit in the front of the jeep."

"What are you talking about, Maarten?"

"We've been liberated, Vera. Don't you realize?"

She is less pleased than I am, but that has always been so. She never was as exuberant in showing her emotions. You always have to spur her on a bit. Therefore I put one arm around her waist.

"Come, let's do a freedom dance."

She takes a few awkward steps with me and then wriggles loose.

"At least Uncle Karel can grow his moustaches again," I chuckle. I feel beautifully warm now. I put the rug over a chair and dig my hands into my pockets.

Vera comes out of the kitchen with a glass. "Here, drink this." At one draught I drain the glass. It makes me warm and drowsy. I sit down on the settee and look in the direction of a sound. A green Chevrolet comes up the drive, followed by a large white Ford. We're having company, just as I am beginning to feel so tired that it seems to be snowing even inside the room. Close my eyes for a moment. Only for a moment.

Another American. I shake his hand cordially. He is called Eardly. Dr. Eardly even. So he's an officer, even though he is in mufti now.

"I've just had a ride in one of your jeeps," I say in fluent English. I had no trouble with that. Very satisfying. Again I grab his hand. Tears spring to my eyes. "If you knew how long we've been waiting for you."

"You have been a bit naughty," says the American. "Walking out of the house without a coat, that's very dangerous at your age."

Come, come, I am not that old. Vera is standing beside him. How small and slender she is compared with him. There have been times these last months when I feared she would become sick, she looked so haggard. At the slightest exertion she had to sit down. I thought there was something wrong with her lungs but it was simply malnutrition. Now we shall soon have plenty to eat again.

"It's cold everywhere," I explain to him. "The only place where you can still get more or less warm is in bed."

Suddenly there is a blonde girl standing in the room. She is wearing a bright red sweater. She doesn't look as if she works in the army. But maybe the American forces have women in civilian dress working for them, secretaries probably. She takes me to another room and tells me to sit down on that bed there. So she is more like a nurse.

"I am actually quite tired," I mutter, while I feel her pulling off my shoes. "It must be the emotion."

She does not reply and starts undressing me. There is no need for that. But she carries on regardless. She is strong and bends my arms back in order to strip off the shirt. Somewhere to the side a door opens. A man with a square face and short-trimmed hair enters with a syringe in his hand. I try to get off the bed but that blonde one holds me down while I feel the needle jab into my arm.

"I want to live! I want to live!!"

"Don't strap him down," I hear a man's voice say. "No need for the straps."

Then I suddenly understand everything. "You've got the wrong man. I wasn't on the wrong side. Maybe I was no hero, but I wasn't on the wrong side. I never hid any fugitives in my house, that is true. I wouldn't have minded, but I never came across any. Or I didn't recognize them in time. Or it was too late, all finished, and I never realized what trouble he was in. Not even afterwards. He was drunk. He was singing. I had no idea. If I had known that the next day . . . maybe he was still drunk when he did it."

Vera comes into the room. Thank God.

"She is my witness. I have never done anything wrong. Isn't that true, Vera? Not even that time in Paris. That wasn't me. That wasn't really me."

She nods reassuringly and sits down on the edge of the bed. Why is she crying? Could it be that I am mistaken and that the war has only just begun? Have we been occupied instead of liberated? Is everything starting all over again?

"Has the war started again?"

"Go to sleep now, Maarten," she says hoarsely. "No one will do you any harm."

"Is there no war?"

"It's peace."

Why is she crying, then? I'm glad she is here. She is the only one I still trust. "You must never leave again," I whisper and take her hand. "Do you hear, Vera, never."

Headache, headache and thirst. Move these lips, maybe words will come back into this head.

Turn the light on! (Good boy.)

What was before this? As if I've come up from a hole in the ice. And so hot. Must get out. (Get out, then!) Wasn't there always someone lying beside you?

Step by step. Luckily there is light burning in this corridor. Wooden floors, straight boards, with joins it would be better to avoid. Watch out for splinters. Pull up your knees, high up!

At the back of this head there's something buzzing. This body is pressing me out. Like a turd I am being pressed out of myself. I can think this with words, but they do not cover what happens. Meanwhile it happens, outside me. (Again an inadequate term.)

The light switch is usually to the right of the door. So it is here. Hi, dog. Wave, don't talk.

It thumps somewhere in my head. (Or is it this house that is making that noise?) I cautiously push the curtain aside, take a few steps back. In the black glass hangs a room, a piano, a desk. An old man in pyjamas looks at me, imitates a live man with his hollow black eyes and his long white thin hands which he now raises, defensively, palms turned outward, to breast level. Quick, close the curtains!

Good God. A man is hovering above the snow out there! A man, a piano, a desk, a whole room floating above the snow out there in the night. Cross the floor to that table over there!

Hi, dog. Licks my hand with his rough tongue. "We must wait till it gets light outside." (Then we can define our position and take the necessary counter-measures.)

A book with a padded cover, a kind of oblong album. (Take the cover between thumb and forefinger, open it!)

Nothing but photographs, black and white ones and color ones. And there is that man in the snow again, only younger. The hatred in those eyes, out there in the snow. No one has ever looked at me like that before. He must go. All pictures of him must go. There's a fireplace over there. Logs are lying beside it, stacked in a potato crate. On the mantelpiece lies a box of matches. Somehow or other I already knew this. Perhaps a case of *déjà vu.*

First tear the photograph carefully from the page and light it and then place it among the wood chips. Small, quivering, yellow-blue flames creeping around the first log. Men sitting in a meeting around a gleaming table. Little bright blue flames along the serrated edges of the photograph where blisters bubble up which pop and then, as they turn chocolate brown, quickly crawl to the middle until the whole meeting room has disappeared.

Pictures of people in a park, people on a beach, that same man again, on the deck of a ship beside a woman who is here standing alone on a rock, laughing, her hair blowing loose. A child in a playpen. A boy and a girl hand in hand posing in front of a bright red swing.

Let them vanish, let them go black and vanish, fly away like dark flakes of soot out through the chimney, turn into black specks in the snow on the roof. I hum softly. The dog beside me likes it, too. At any rate, he is lying with his head between his forepaws beside me and watches my hands as they pick the photographs out of the album and drop them one by one in the crackling, smoking fire.

Two women, two women in rustling garments, a young one and an older one. They speak English and take a book of photographs out of my hands. (Better do what they want, I'm no longer as strong as I was, seriously weakened, as it turns out.)
Get up. The throbbing starts again. Dizzy. And thirst. Don't want to go outside between them. (Do they want to turn me out because I am becoming too difficult?) "Not to that man in the snow!"

Yet another room. How many rooms are there around me? I am being turned over. They strap me down. Undoubtedly as a precaution. Everything here is in movement. Like on a ship. Amazing that those two stay on their feet. They say nothing. Hard, closed, women's faces under artificial light. Resolute, overconcentrated, busy. Every wrinkle and crease becomes rigid in this merciless light. It is utterly silent, apart from the throbbing which is now close behind my eyes.
"Something wet on my head, please."
I get it at once. Coolness seeping in through my skull. Water runs into my mouth. I suck at it greedily.

Am alone now. How silent it is. Where has the world gone? Gently shake this head. Shake everything out of it. (Maybe one will then become again who one was before?) Through a chink in the curtains, somewhere over there, appears a thin strip of hesitant light. Seem to feel that this body has become light. (Atmospheric changes? Vanished thoughts? Spring coming perhaps?)

No way back, no way forward. Fill this space more and more. (Breathe as little as possible, therefore, so as not to expand even more in the emptiness around me.)

There is a cloth, somewhere above my eyes, but I cannot reach it. Am stuck. Maybe I am not really large at all, but small, maybe I have lost the sense of my own dimensions. Don't know. Is that why they have tied me down, are they afraid I will fall out of bed with this enormous head?

Shake gently, no words, only humming, melodies skimming close above the ground, humming like bees, bumblebees above the grass. Humming against throbbing. Still and yet moving. Less and less body, specific weight. And full of heavy water, which somewhere down below seeks a way out in a warm stream.

Don't . . . don't . . . don't undo. (Have become as light as air.) Don't. (Yet it is done.)

Grab hold of me, great sharpness hurting my hands. It smarts between those legs as they walk, or rather are dragged, to a tiled space full of steam. Can't see a thing.

It's better like this, warm water and nothing to be seen. Behind the steam questions are being asked. I can tell they are questions and I nod. Nod . . . just nod. It gets across.

"Water all right?"

Yesyes, water all right, we nod. Let me sink. Like him.

Arm hoisting me up under my armpits. Up we go. Careful, I have become so light all of a sudden.

"Lots of clothes!"

Get nothing but a bathrobe, belt tied around me.

Through doors. How many? And all those directions, enough to make you dizzy.

"Up to the North!" My voice still sounds distinct, still does, but much feebler. (Wear and tear?)

Vera's hand. (Surely that is her hand?) Don't take your eyes off now, follow now, until a large, flat area of wood comes into view, a smooth, gleaming expanse, in front of which you are set down, seated, bent double. Hold on to wood, this thick wooden edge. Otherwise you will rise or capsize.

Now it is also in the words themselves. Light sentences come first, shoot up like corks, intended or unintended, the better sentences are too long and too heavy, they go on hovering somewhere under my tongue. This is eating. Can eat by myself, honestly, am no longer a little baby. Eating . . . lots . . . lots. No time for cutlery which clatters out of sight into the depths beneath me. Quickly stuff it into my mouth. (Before they take it all away again, start polishing me up, rub my cheeks with a rough cloth.)

Light hollows out. Human beings are so full of holes. Human beings should be more closed. In the end you can't keep anything inside any more.

Lovely smooth wood to rub. Movement which prevents emptying. Better not look aside either. Straight ahead, those eyes!

Voices calling that it is snowing again. Your back towards it. Don't tolerate any more fluttering.

Am moved once again. (Question: "Can you walk by yourself?") Could, but a little too dangerous just now.

Leaning heavily on that mohair arm. Let go. Fall. A tumble into a hard chair. Wood on either side. Wooden slats around my body.

Grab hold of them, again the chasing flakes outside that I can't help seeing now. There is thick snow on the blue roof of Vera's Datsun. (This was one of those old-fashioned, good old heavy rows of words.)

Persevere, find the happy mean between rising and sinking in yourself. Congeal around a center, a center of gravity.

Question: "How are you feeling?"
    A question that can be answered. Wait a moment. Wave briefly with those hands. Like this. Only very briefly. Quickly grab hold of the wood again. Wait a moment. "Not enough gravity!"

Wind drawing patterns and whirling about in the flakes; drawing streaks and stripes across the window panes. Winter falls deeper and deeper (and there is less and less that one can set against it). Judging by the snowflakes the wind now comes from all sides.

One thing: don't go to sleep now. Don't fall asleep. Would like to. Mustn't, though. Hold head straight! Make a firm stand! Preparedness! (Pre-war word, blown over from Pop's world to here, to this head which has become much too large to go on living in.)

Beside me a girl in a fluffy, soft-blue pullover. She looks at the snow. She paints her lips. She holds a little mirror up to her face. (The actions possess a faint echo of cohesion.) Suddenly there is such loud laughter in me that everything begins to shake around me and one hand slips away from the arm of the chair with quick, grab-eager fingers in the direction of a blinking little mirror. I look into it. Away with it! Someone takes it from my lap and lays a hand on this ever-swelling head. Of course, he or she notices it too. It's a hydrocephalus. (Can't you feel how light you have become? Soon you will rise to the surface.)

One is being pushed aside. They have brought in someone else. I have been able to see that in a mirror just now. One must develop counter-pressure. (But how can counter-pressure be developed from a void?) Somewhere there must still be some energy available, somewhere in Maarten Klein there must still be a Maarten Klein, surely?

A brush on wood, a stain on the floor, they provide no duration, only a state. (There's no connection any more in anything around here, dammit.)

Words, that's what provides energy, they are themselves energy. A human being should be made of words. Totally. It's so obvious. (At last something of worth again, supply of words there must be, that's what can save the situation, stories, supply, import of stories.)

"Read to me!"

Movement starts up in the room. (You see, when you use the right words something always happens.) A young woman with long blonde hair disappears through an open door. Can see her back slipping away. Another woman takes her place, front forward. A pleasant old voice she has, slightly faltering.

"Read!"

Follow her in the space around this chair. See a book being picked up from the table. Book. Words. I eagerly stretch out my hands towards it. I hug and stroke the book. A man in a raincoat and hat. He looks up at a hill with palms, and a brightly lit hotel on it. The title is unfamiliar to me, and so are the words. I return the book to the lady.

Now I hear English, the English language. Perhaps it is better so. Only sounds, sounds and rhythm. Cool, bright, unfathomable. An old woman's voice, trembling and thin, rising and falling, sometimes to the rhythm of the snowflakes outside the window until a fresh gust of wind disturbs the equilibrium between the flakes and the voice. The voice brings movement closer, progress from sentence to sentence. I hear names recur and that amusing play of rising and falling, of question and answer. Then it stops. The voice has gone and everything goes dead.

Am alone again in this space. Squeeze the wooden chair arms with these fingers. On one hand (not this one but that one) is a little scab. (Pick at it.)

An even older woman, her brown hair pinned up, wearing a black high-necked dress. (She is as complete as you could wish the image of a person to be.) She sits down facing me and says the picking should stop, it shouldn't be done, she says. "Otherwise you become lost."

A small round drop of blood on the back of this, no, of that hand. Rub it out to as large a stain as possible. Squeeze hard. And again. There's another drop.

"You see. As long as blood flows there is still hope."

She seems to understand that. She nods with a smile around her lips, which purse as they suddenly approach fast. Ugh! I quickly turn my head away, rub over that damp spot on my cheek. (If they start slobbering at you, where will it end.)

Flakes. Plural. There is only plural in the world, multiplication, the world expands more and more. (I understand all about that demonstration out there but don't want to join in, don't take part, one shouldn't let oneself be swept along into that faceless fluttering out there.) Shut your eyes! But it goes on snowing. It snows even inside me. No more defense anywhere.

□

A doorbell. Someone who wants to come in from outside. That is what that sound means, you can be sure. Someone wants to come in. He or she rings the bell. The door is opened.

A long white car stands in front of the veranda. I hear voices, male voices and thumping shoes.

They all stand there, out of nowhere, suddenly, just like that, tall as houses, a circle of people around me. Men in white jackets with a red emblem on the breast pocket. I want to hold on to my chair but feel no strength anywhere. Watch how they unhook old fingers one by one from the arms of a chair.

Am lifted, slid into a bed with straps, tied down, lifted, I hang aslant in the room. (Men, hold on tight, you have no idea how light is your burden.)

Furniture, piano, an entire interior, a whole room totters and tilts past me. Vera stands by the door. "Vera!" I want to raise myself, hanging at a slant I stretch out my arms towards her. "Vera!" Am stuck fast, fettered. They carry me out of the door and I call out to her, "Vera!", but I no longer see her and am again tilted through a doorway and lie crying in the snow, flakes land on my lips, on my cheeks, and I see her once more, she looks at a thermometer behind a window and then the white doors of the ambulance close and the driving begins in this rocking car which is also a ship Vera and also a snowflake in which I lie tied down and which skims past tree tops where other snowflakes chase along with us, accompany us like falling stars and so we fall through space Vera and glimmer briefly afterwards (or are we already dead) until we fade away or burn out, become white flakes, or black specks, what's the difference?

Question of mistake or exchange? . . . a tall bare space with concrete flower troughs full of pitch-black earth . . . no flowers only scuffed kitchen chairs . . . men and women in mouse-grey overalls . . . sometimes distant, sometimes frighteningly near.

   SUDDENLY THEY ARE STANDING BEFORE ME

deportation? . . . only English is spoken here . . . through large windows: a view of a tall brick wall topped with upright green bits of glass . . . so these people are hidden from the eye of the world . . . what happens to them? . . . the guards are dressed in white with dark blue neckties, both men and women . . . are clearly under instruction not to listen . . . I come from the Netherlands, the only one here . . . vomit—long and plaintive—as if the person can scarcely muster the strength for it . . . once again someone spewing himself inside out.

In the snow-covered courtyard stands a birch, spindly branches end in fine, motionless twigs, dark patches on the thin twisted trunk, a

   BIRCH

it still has that word and therefore I still see you beloved . . .

Such people's faces are white as sheets and show nothing . . . masks in a museum . . . perhaps it is an exhibition, a competition in sitting still?

Loud school bell, several times in a row . . . chatter breaks out on all sides . . . a voice cries softly . . . another voice crooning the same tune all the time . . . it seems spontaneous but it is mechanical.

□

A birch surrounded by snow ... if only I could be where that birch is ...

HERE YOU ARE!

A big sheet of white paper ... a hand ... a woman's hand ... a woman's hand holding a wooden box ... a box divided into sections, upright partitions ... a scent rises from it, right across the daffodils ... two scents floating around me ... flowing into each other ... flowers and graphite ... together a name ... sweetest and heaviest word of my life ... rises from the bottom-most depth like an air bubble ... escapes and bursts resoundingly asunder ... I slam my hand in front of my mouth and bite my fingers.

THAT'S OK. DRAW VERA'S PORTRAIT. THAT'S JUST FINE, THAT'S OK FOR US.

Out of here ... don't know from which side the world is coming towards me ... there must surely be a direction? ... every space must have an entrance and an exit, mustn't it?

Hands ... feet ... scraping of scuffed chair legs across concrete ... want one Mr. Klein to say "Vera," say it, VeraVeraVeraVeraVeraVera until I hear it ... hear how my voice drifts away ... gone is gone.

Much singing and crooning from all nooks and crannies ... faces: battered ... stretched ... bloated ... flaky (and more such words).

Lightly undulating ... the whole inside now threatens to come out ... Einstein was right once but he forgot this place ... light has no longer any velocity here ... nothing for me to enjoy.

□

Can that smell of piss clear off!

They shine lamps at you in here . . . probably to see what is still lying here . . . what has been left in my eyes . . . what may still move a little . . . they want to have it all . . . grasp everything they can get . . . so he is being slowly scooped empty here, the Maarten that was.

YOU'RE MR. KLEIN?
the birch in the snow . . . it can't help me either . . . I am led away . . . wave one last time . . . shall never see her again.

A white corridor with a green line half-way up the wall . . . very slow, solemn walking held by one arm (and by the line on the wall).

Utterly loose in space . . . girl with reddish-brown curly hair very close by now . . . the sun sparkles in the outer hairs around her head . . . space . . . sink at once . . . feel ground . . . they don't understand why someone who is so empty must lie down here . . . they understand nothing of what I say . . . the thought of an interpreter doesn't occur to them . . . I am the only survivor of my own language.

People sit in long rows on benches and wooden seats . . . women and men . . . drugged it would seem from the way they sit staring in front of them at the whitewashed wall.

Smell of paper, cardboard, glue, wood . . . good smells . . . those people bending over are they asleep? . . . high up in the ceiling there is music slowly trickling down . . . tables covered in colorful strips of paper, glue-pots, brushes ... party hat rolled onto its side ... red with a green pompom at the top.

It's stuffy here ... fresher atmosphere would be desirable ... my footsteps on the floor can no longer be felt ... soles too thick, floor too soft, who or what is to tell? ... feeling is no longer passed on ... remains hanging somewhere halfway ... counterpressure ... soft compulsion ... sit.

WE'RE GOING TO MAKE A DRAWING TODAY. A SELF PORTRAIT. WOULD YOU LIKE TO DO IT IN PENCIL OR WOULD YOU RATHER USE PAINT, MR. KLEIN?

A woman's voice ebbing away into a question mark ... scent moves from place to place ... the air has become almost too thin for smells ... a hand holding scissors cuts slowly in the air.

LET'S GIVE IT A TRY

Flower scent ... daffodils ... so spring must have come ... without him having noticed.

Beam of light full of dancing dust specks ... proof once more that light itself stands still ... perhaps this is the discovery of your life ... the goal.

As soon as singing, shouting, chattering breaks out, the light becomes denser ... everyone hopes to be home before dark.

From behind a stick prodding me in the back ... straight away give a kick backwards without looking round ... bellowing! ... on your knees you! ... kneel!

Hands and feet it must have ... eyes open and shut: same place ... eyes open and shut and open again: same place.

□

Thick, greasy smell is born or carried in ... hangs sweating everywhere ... the doors are deliberately kept shut with clanging keys ... they seem to need music with everything here ... this in imitation of time if you ask him ... farts are the only remedy against it ... utmost disapproval ... a sound that is usually accompanied by hilarity ... but for hilarity one needs a head and nobody here has that any more.

They come past ... they are on their way ... stand still ... not allowed ... changes are clearly no longer permitted ... sit with a big head which from sheer emptiness hangs forward ... caught hard by the edge of a table ... and laughing!

Look, this is not exactly humor ... humor is when someone trips on a banana skin ... comic is when someone sees a banana skin and gives it a wide berth and ends up in the path of a falling brick ... big lump ... head which is clearly so conspicuous here that they keep fussing about it ... especially women or what passes as such ... away, you witches!

All the time he needs to keep human beings at arm's length ... someone sings ... very wonderful but hidden behind a pillar ... and why not ... why not admit to everything: that there are voices without bodies. They make sure that people always take everything with them when they are dragged from place to place.

There are still hands and feet on him but hardly controlled ... spoon ... fork ... still knows more or less what this has to do with eating and so on ... steering is seriously inspired ... steaming food lies all over the place ... a plate ... the rim is smooth and round to the fingers ... things keep being taken away in order to prevent one from settling down here . . . complete disorientation, that is the aim . . . deliberately refuse to understand that this plate is a prop, an anchor for his fingers.

Don't understand anyone . . . only the familiar words . . . his own language from within . . . both his parents spoke Dutch . . . they are both dead now . . . everyone he knows seems to be dead . . . do you know . . . you astray amid this herd . . . you are the only ray of hope.

Tucking in . . . beside . . . across . . . opposite . . . don't even know why they are being fed, the stupid hogs . . . namely to retain any weight at all . . . hence the rumpus when suddenly someone sits down to shit . . . quite understand those guards . . . a) it is filthy . . . b) they would blow away on the merest breeze.

Too far removed from the wall . . . which is bad . . . a body that can no longer propel itself becomes a tree . . . like that thin one over there in the snow . . . the wall . . . to the wall . . . over the wall . . . that is what he means when he thinks: only in language can I still undertake anything.

Still hands but once out of sight they snap off . . . fall away . . . once out of sight they can no longer be felt either . . . how heavy I am . . . heavy nothingness. Back into life? . . . but where has it gone? . . . is there such a thing? . . . or was everything simply a fantasy in the head? . . . phantoms of the mind?

At least pinching still causes a slight pain . . . an event . . . using the choke but where has the engine gone . . . nothing but metaphors, boy . . . nothing but metaphors.

□

The head rolls about on the neck all by itself without any guidance ... must try to shrink ... at any rate this boy here must not eat any more.

Shuffle those feet down there ... rub with those hands higher up ... help to crush this little person in between ... into his disappearance ... that is what they do to all these people here ...

Don't care for anything at all, don't care ... grasping ... holding ... letting go is now done independently by this hand like a machine which he watches.

Extinguished male head ... dribble running into the collar of his overalls ... pink lips opening and closing as those of a fish ... drums absently with his fingers on his flies ... am I like that, too?

The garden wall is good ... imitate a wall, most of the people here do that and who can blame them? ... some of them have quite a talent for it.

Sounds do not remain constant or does the head lower its hearing at times?

A madhouse? ... think: not mad means nothing ... one can't check for oneself whether one is mad or not.

Far in the distance there is gunfire ... shots ... fine business that is, there's even a war on now ... will it never end? ... occupied from within ... my liberators have occupied me, that's what it is ... more and more censorship ... hardly anything still gets through.

□

Sick ... sick as anything ... but can't tell whether the sickness is inside or outside this skin ... on the borderline there is not a breath of air ... he has become a thin, transparent point in space.

Tea in metal mugs ... warms the hands ... lukewarm never becomes hot ... but hot does become lukewarm ... can this be called progress while in fact it is regression ... to a state in which everything ends up having the same temperature ... tea can never of its own accord become colder than its surroundings ... that is so ... the static condition of tea for which stirring is of no further avail ... let go that mug because those hands down there ... those stiff fingers ... serve no purpose any longer ... on the contrary ... they freeze everything they touch.

    MR. BRACKEEN! HOW DELIGHTFUL TO SEE YOU!

Poor thing ... pitiful really.

This is the best corner ... at last ... little human traffic ... occasionally someone accidentally strays this way and is immediately barked at ... that one over there is a metronome ... left ... right ... at every turn he clicks his tongue ... rhythmically swings back and forth in his chair like the pendulum of a clock ... of course, you could start laughing at it but it is too understandable for that (vertical wants to become horizontal ... but all you do here is sink, boy).

Still louder music ... two starting to dance with each other ... bending and in stockinged feet they dance around each other ... very carefully they hold hands ... in a moment their fingers will break off.

A woman slumps to the ground against a wall ... slowly like treacle along the wall ... she claps and she cries ... tears streaming while

she laughs ... loudly and a stream of tears down her cheeks and
she claps her hands harder and harder and then
SUDDENLY
as if at a signal
SHE TURNS TO STONE
with a purple face that slowly becomes ashen grey ... they can
carry that one away he thinks and this is exactly what happens.

Walking dozily ... shuffling ... his shoes are gone ... that is why
he no longer has any feeling in his feet ... breathing is in the head
now ... has struck inside ... a rustling rising and falling.

Can it be they have found him somewhere ... a strange country
and his passport lost or his memory or both ... no papers ... that
they are sorting it out ... who he is and what his name is and
where he comes from ... only: it no longer interests me so obviously
they stop their investigations and will leave me here until the end,
anonymous for all time.

Eyes fill with prickly water ... silting up? ... cheeks are already
caked with salt.

Everybody has been brought here in order to be emptied by means
of medicine ... the lost-property department is already so overfull
that everything that lands on the floor is at once deposited in
garbage cans ... this does not apply to this person here who handed
in all his remaining possessions at the entrance.

From the corner of the eye: a person pulling out his last tuft of
hair because even that is too much for him ... poke about a
bit ... rummage in these pockets so as not to have to see too much.

□

Light flickers down at me from tubes up above . . . light that wants to penetrate every hollow . . . close tightly . . . keep shut . . . lock up . . . he pulls the door shut behind him for good and at the same time long white trailing curtains close off the view of the wall . . . the spindly tree in the snow.

Sit motionless and yet the feeling of forming part of a larger movement . . . not perceptible . . . a mussel under the keel of a sailing ship.

All around you the last remnants of humanity are being played out . . . a grin on a stubbly old man's mug returns every other second . . . don't look at this human clockface any longer . . . better stroll about for a bit but they have weighted down his legs . . . for your own good . . . we no longer weigh anything here.

A woman grinding coffee at a table with a begonia on it . . . she does not have the use of a coffee grinder but her movements are so lifelike that you can smell the coffee . . . people only imitate here . . . they cling to their last remembered remnants . . . but why so many sit waving to each other (to each other?) is a mystery to me . . . don't join in this game of false identities . . . one must have sunk or strayed very far if one raises every random stranger to friend just so as not to be so alone here.

YOU'RE THE NEW ONE?
in so far as you can still speak of new here . . . oh, are we going to the canteen . . . didn't know that was here.

Large color photographs hang in wooden frames . . . a beach with wild breakers . . . palm trees with a row of canoes underneath . . .

New York at night . . . made to sit down at one of the Formica tables . . . they have a lot of canteen staff here . . . the coffee turns up without delay.

Everyone is given pills in round plastic cups . . . the coffee lady peers at a list for a long time.

I'M THE NEW ONE

you shouldn't have said that . . . a woman with a horribly scraggy neck and a child's bolero made of remnants of wool wants to know your name now . . . he shakes his head but the hag insists with her high shrill voice . . . a bald gentleman in a crookedly buttoned cardigan tries to be helpful with pen and paper but he does not concede his identity and as he stubbornly goes on stirring his coffee he thinks: better forget that too . . . then your alibi will be altogether watertight.

Singing here and there . . . worn voices trying to follow a piano on a stage playing much too fast . . . he is clearly the only one to register that no one is playing on it . . . the price one pays these days for a bit of social life! . . . the utterly moronic community singing to which the fat canteen boss sweating in his white shirt on the stage tries in a loud voice to incite the dozy company before him.

Get up, you . . . go and inspect that piano from close by . . . he walks to the little steps by the side of the stage . . . toilingly clambers up . . . keys that go up and down all by themselves . . . now in the middle register then in a rapidly ascending run in the descant . . . perhaps they can help your fingers . . . teach them perhaps to play again . . . to play from memory again . . . that blissful feeling that your body is playing you . . . that you yourself have become music . . . he sits down on the chair in front of the piano and feels the keys knocking against his fingers . . . they push you away . . .

rebuff you ... won't have anything more to do with you and the canteen boss with his grinning face pulls you off the chair and wants you to help drill those grey old people at those tables down below to the beat of the shrill automatic piano behind you which strikes up "Home on the Range" and he sees the childlike abandonment on all those singing, wide-open faces that are so happy at being allowed to do the same thing together on the orders of the music machine.

Run away then ... away from here and you grope your way among the thick folds of a back curtain ... with the laughter from the hall in your ears you fumble ... grab hold of the folds ... clawing along the curtain until you have found the way out and stand panting in the darkness where you can still hear the piano but more muffled and also the singing feebler and poorer ... he is searching for the exit ... that's what I like to see ... and ends up by the steps again down which you climb or stumble, it isn't certain which, and then you see light burning at the end of a corridor with a freestone floor and tall, barred windows and past a row of toilets without doors ... then he enters a space with washstands and taps ... the drinking troughs ... here is water at last ... drink ... go on drinking ... rinse ... rinse ... rinse ... stream ... I must stream ... lie under water and stream along ... stream away ... why do those guards remove this body from its fountainhead and dry it and lead it away from the water?

They take it to a space where there are beds ... they make it sit on the edge of a bed ... they undress it ... they put pyjamas on it that look like the pyjamas of those other men with their big, staring, half-bald heads on the tall, white pillows and all turned towards him ... they push a pill into his throat ... they pour water through it as if he were a funnel ... they lay him in the bed ... they walk past the row of beds together ... they are silent until they reach the door and call out together good night GOOD NIGHT they call and then it is dark.

There is breathing everywhere ... they have all come here to sleep for the last time together ... who with whom no longer matters ... no more names ... no more faces ... only breathing ... sighing ... all of them known to him when they were still alive ... each one of them ... name and surname ... she is among them somewhere ... seek her ... her hand we must seek ... this takes time ... a whole lifetime it takes ... breathing out and sighing and groaning and wailing and whimpering and snoring ... her hand will come to you ... here ... first take that hand that gropes aimlessly in the dark ... take it gently ... calm him ... now you no longer need to hold anything yourself ... she will do that from now on ... she carries you ... I carry you ... little boy of mine ... the whole long frightening night I will carry you until it is light again.

When it is already light and GOOD MORNING and someone says ... whispers ... the voice of a woman and you listen—you listen with closed eyes ... listen only to her voice whispering ... that the window has been repaired ... that where first that old door had been nailed ... there is glass again ... glass you can see through ... outside ... into the woods and the spring that is almost beginning ... she says ... she whispers ... the spring which is about to begin ...

OUT OF MIND
has been set by NK Graphics
in a Linotron 202 version of Granjon.
Named after the great French printer, designer,
and punch-cutter, Robert Granjon, the face was designed
for the Linotype Corporation by George W. Jones and was first
issued by them in 1924. Based on the sixteenth-century types used
by Claude Garamond, Granjon more closely resembles Garamond's
own type than do any of the various modern types that bear his
name. It remains to this day one of the most enduring and
beautiful of the classic faces recut for modern use in the
early decades of this century. This book was printed
and bound by the Maple-Vail Book Manufacturing
Group, Binghamton, New York. Designed
by Lisa Clark